*Starry,
Starry
Night*

You'll want to read these inspiring novels by

One Last Wish novels:

Mourning Song
A Time to Die
Mother, Help Me Live
Someone Dies, Someone Lives
Sixteen and Dying
Let Him Live
The Legacy: Making Wishes Come True
Please Don't Die
She Died Too Young
All the Days of Her Life
A Season for Goodbye

The Dawn Rochelle Quartet:

Six Months to Live
I Want to Live
So Much to Live For
No Time to Cry

Other novels by Lurlene McDaniel:

Angels Watching Over Me
Lifted Up by Angels
Until Angels Close My Eyes
Till Death Do Us Part
For Better, for Worse, Forever
I'll Be Seeing You
Saving Jessica
Don't Die, My Love
Too Young to Die
Goodbye Doesn't Mean Forever
Somewhere Between Life and Death
Time to Let Go
Now I Lay Me Down to Sleep
When Happily Ever After Ends
Baby Alicia Is Dying

**From every ending
comes a new beginning. . . .**

Lurlene McDaniel

Starry, Starry Night

Three Holiday Stories

BANTAM BOOKS
NEW YORK • TORONTO • LONDON • SYDNEY • AUCKLAND

Published by
Bantam Books
Bantam Doubleday Dell Publishing Group, Inc.
1540 Broadway
New York, New York 10036

Bantam Books are published by Bantam Books, a division of
Bantam Doubleday Dell Publishing Group, Inc. Its trademark,
consisting of the words "Bantam Books" and the portrayal of a
rooster, is Registered in U.S. Patent and Trademark Office and in
other countries. Marca Registrada.

Library of Congress Cataloging-in-Publication Data

McDaniel, Lurlene.
   Starry, starry night / by Lurlene McDaniel.
      p.   cm.
   Contents: Starry, starry night—Last dance—Kathy's life.
   Summary: A collection of three stories in which teenagers face
life-altering situations.
ISBN 0-553-57130-3
   1. Children's stories, American.   [1. Short stories.]   I. Title.
PZ7.M47841St   1998
[Fic]—dc21
                                                        98-13372
                                                        CIP
                                                        AC

The text of this book is set in 12-point Adobe Cochin.
Book design by Susan Clark
Manufactured in the United States of America
November 1998
        10 9 8 7 6 5

To all the dreamers —
may your wishes all come true.

Contents

*"I am the Root and the Offspring of David,
and the bright Morning Star."*

REVELATION 22:16
(NEW INTERNATIONAL VERSION)

Magi from the east came to Jerusalem and asked, "Where is the one who has been born king of the Jews? We saw his star in the east and have come to worship him." . . . and the star they had seen in the east went ahead of them until it stopped over the place where the child was. When they saw the star, they were overjoyed.

MATTHEW 2:2, 9–10
(NEW INTERNATIONAL VERSION)

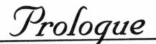

Prologue

Everyone has wished upon a star.

The young, the old, dreamers all—and even those who have been disappointed.

One can always hope.

You know the words:

> *Star light, star bright,*
> *First star I see tonight,*
> *I wish I may, I wish I might*
> *Have the wish I wish tonight.*

These whispered wishes tossed to the heavens are only for the ears of angels. So remember to be careful what you wish for. Indeed, your wish may be granted, but not always in the way you had imagined.

Come now. Hear three wishes made on a starry, starry night . . . wishes made from the heart, with only angels listening.

Book One

CHRISTMAS
CHILD

One

"**M**om, look at these. Aren't they cute?" Melanie Barton jiggled a pair of dinosaur-shaped baby booties under her mother's nose. Melanie and her mother, Connie, stood in a baby superstore, surrounded by aisles of adorable merchandise. Her mother leaned heavily against a shopping cart heaped with diapers, newborn-size clothes, crib sheets, and a mobile and eyed the bright dino booties.

"Yes, they're cute, but I think they're too big for a newborn. Your feet weren't any bigger than this." Connie held out her finger and thumb to indicate a couple of inches, then arched her back and rubbed the hollow "I need to get off my feet, Mellie. I'd forgot ten how much your back aches when you're pregnant."

"How about the paint store? You said we could stop there before we go home. I need more yellow to finish the nursery walls."

"You'll get it done before the baby comes, I'm sure. Right now, I want to get home before I collapse."

"But I still have Christmas shopping to do."

"It'll keep, Mellie," her mother said pa tiently. "I need to rest. You can go to the mall anytime."

Melanie told herself to be sensitive to her pregnant mother. In only a couple more weeks, Melanie's little brother or sister would be born. Since Christmas was also only two weeks away, it was possible that the baby could be born on Christmas Day. Which was what Melanie was secretly hop ing.

"If only I could drive," Melanie grumbled as she and her mother walked to the car, pushing the cart full of purchases.

"This time next year you'll have your li

cense, and you can take Baby Mortimer Christmas shopping while I sit around eating candy and reading a book."

Suddenly Melanie stopped. "You and Dad aren't really going to call him Mortimer, are you?"

Her mother laughed. "Don't be silly. It could be a girl. Then we'll call her Morticia."

"Mother! Don't joke. We can't give the baby some crazy name. It has to be something special."

"I'm sure you have some suggestions."

"A few."

"Can you save them for later? I just want to get home and lie down."

On the drive home, Melanie gazed at the Christmas decorations hung from lampposts, the store windows decked out with lights, glitter, and holiday displays of toys and clothes. Santas stood on street corners, ringing bells and collecting money. Outside, the world looked expectant, ready for the most wonderful day of the year. Inside, Melanie's heart felt full to overflowing. What a Christmas this was going to be!

In the spring, when her mother had first told Melanie about her pregnancy, Melanie had been shocked, then embarrassed. Weren't her parents too old? Forty-two and forty-five seemed pretty old to be having a baby. And she had wondered what her friends would think. As it turned out, her friends thought she was lucky to be getting a newborn baby to cuddle and hold. Now she couldn't wait.

Back at the house, Melanie unloaded the car. "You go lie down," she told her mother once they were in the foyer. "I can start dinner."

Her mother patted Melanie's cheek. "You've been such a help to me. I don't know what I'd do without you, honey."

"I guess it's one of the perks of having babies fifteen years apart," Melanie said with a grin.

Her mother headed upstairs. "Let me know when your dad gets home. Remind him that we have Lamaze class tonight."

Melanie had to hand it to her parents. Despite their age, they were going all out to make this birth a memorable experience. They were attending natural-childbirth classes at the local hospital where their baby would be born. Melanie had even gone with

hem a couple of times. The class was full of
young couples, and although her parents
ooked old among them, the group had wel-
comed them warmly.

"We always wanted a big family," Melanie
had overheard her mom tell one woman.
'But after Melanie's birth, I just couldn't
seem to get pregnant again. Imagine my
shock when it happened now, after all these
years!"

In the kitchen, Melanie quickly got to
work making dinner. A casserole was warm-
ing in the oven and she was starting on the
salad when the phone rang.

"What's shaking?" It was the voice of her
friend Coren.

"Just slaving in the kitchen. What's up
with you?" Melanie cradled the phone beneath her chin and broke lettuce into a salad
bowl.

"Nothing," Coren said with an exagger-
ated sigh. School was out for the holidays
and she already sounded bored. "Are you
going to Justine's party next Saturday?"

"It depends on how my mom's doing."

"She's okay, isn't she?"

"Sure, but she says that sometimes babies

arrive early, so the baby could be here b
Saturday."

"But you've *got* to come."

"I will if I can." Melanie didn't see why
was so urgent that she go.

"Well, try hard, all right?"

Changing the subject, Melanie said, "Yo
should see all the cute stuff we bought fo
the baby today. The clothes are so tiny. It'
be like dressing a doll." She heard her fa
ther's key in the door. "Got to run. My dad'
home. I'll call you tomorrow." Melanie hun
up and kissed her father's cheek as he cam
into the room.

"Where's your mom?"

"Upstairs, resting."

He swiped a piece of carrot from the cut
ting board and ruffled her hair, which irri
tated her. "Smells good in here."

"Mom said to remind you about Lamaz
class tonight. Can you drop me at the mal
on your way there and pick me up on you
way home?"

Her father set down his briefcase. "You
know I hate you wandering the mall alone.

"Dad, there's a thousand people at th
mall. It's not like I'll get lost or anything."

"You could get mugged."

She rolled her eyes, ignoring his concern. "I still have Christmas shopping to do, and Mom said it was all right with her."

"I'll discuss it with your mom."

"I'm not a baby, you know."

"But you're still my baby," he said with a grin.

"I can get everything done before your class is over. Promise." Melanie made a final stab at pleading her case.

"I said we'll discuss it, Mellie. Now I'm going upstairs."

Melanie pouted. She'd be glad when the baby was here and her father could see what a *real* baby looked like. She was tired of him always treating her as if she were still five. It was about time he started treating her like the fifteen-year-old she was. It was part of the hazard of being an only child, she reminded herself. Her friends always got to try new things ahead of her. But her own parents were usually the last ones to okay anything she wanted to do.

Still sulking, Melanie carried the garbage pail onto the back porch. The frosty air felt cold on her warm cheeks She looked up.

The sky was dark, but in the west she could still see a hint of lavender and pink left from the setting sun. A single star twinkled, as if trapped between the light and the darkness. Impulsively she said, "Star light, star bright, first star I see tonight . . ." Finishing the familiar children's rhyme, she asked, "Could I have a baby sister? And if it's not too much trouble, do you think you could get my parents to treat me as a truly older sister and let the new baby be the baby?"

The star winked like a tiny jeweled eye, making her think that perhaps it had heard her and would grant her wishes.

Two

Coren came over on Saturday afternoon to help Melanie finish the nursery. Melanie's father had assembled the crib that morning. Now Melanie was putting on the sheets while Coren stacked diapers in a diaper bag decorated with tiny giraffes. "What's next?" Coren asked.

"I bought a bunch of stars to paste on the ceiling for the baby to look at," Melanie told her. "You can't see them in the daytime, but at night they glow Whenever she looks up, she'll think she's seeing the universe. Clever, huh?"

"Totally awesome. You keep saying 'she.'"

"Wishful thinking. I'd really like a sister."

"You can have mine!"

Melanie had listened to Coren's complaints about her older sister for years. The two of them never seemed to get along. "Cheer up. Next year she'll go to college, so you'll have the bathroom all to yourself."

Coren chuckled. "You'll only have to share your bathroom with poopy diapers, not a mirror hog."

Melanie fit the bumper pad around the inside of the crib. "I'll probably be going off to college myself just about the time baby sis—or bro—is walking and talking. I'll miss everything cute she does and says."

"I'll send my brother over. You can listen to him all you want."

"No, thanks. Ten-year-old brothers probably don't have anything to say that I want to hear."

"How true. But don't sweat it. At least you'll be around when the baby's at its sweetest and cutest. A tiny baby . . . lucky you!"

Melanie did feel lucky. She unpacked the

mobile that she and her mother had picked out together and attached it to the side of the crib. She wound it up and listened to it play "Twinkle, Twinkle, Little Star."

"That's cute," Coren said. The two friends watched the tiny moons and stars rotate on colored strings. "Maybe the baby will like something more upbeat" Coren suggested. "Maybe some rock '

Melanie made a face 'No way. Mom only plays classical music for the baby."

"As if it could hear it."

"It *can* hear. Her doctor said that babies can hear while they're still inside, and they can recognize their mother's voice once they're born."

"No way."

"It's true! I've been reading one of Mom's books so I should know."

"Well, how do those doctors know this stuff? It's not like a baby can tell them anything."

"Research," Melanie said. "And classical music is supposed to make babies smarter too."

"So what are you wearing to Justine's party tonight?" Coren changed the subject

'My red sweater and jeans. How about you?" Melanie had decided to go to the party, since the doctor had told her mother during her last checkup that the baby's birth wasn't imminent. Melanie was glad. Every day her mom stayed pregnant increased the chance that she might have the baby on Christmas Day.

"How are you two doing?" Melanie's mother came into the nursery and looked around. "Girls, this is lovely. And the yellow walls make it look so cheerful."

Pleased by her mother's reaction, Melanie said, "What do you think of the dresser?" She'd chosen a handful of stickers depicting characters from fairy tales and stuck them to the freshly painted white chest of drawers.

"You've done a fine job, Mellie, and I really appreciate it. I haven't had much energy this past month. If it hadn't been for you, the little guy would be sleeping in a very ugly room." She grinned. "Now why don't you and Coren come have some Christmas cookies, hot from the oven."

"Race you," Melanie said.

Like a shot, the two girls darted from the room and down the stairs.

❋   ❋   ❋

"Surprise!"

Melanie stared at the small circle of her friends in Justine's family room. Bewildered, she asked, "What's going on? It's not my birthday or anything."

"We're having a big-sister shower for you," Coren explained, looking pleased. "We bought presents and everything."

"I made the cake," Mindy called out.

"And I bought the ice cream," Lorna added.

"You're kidding! You're giving me a party?"

"Yep." Justine gestured at the others. "Some of us are experts on being a big sister. I thought we should show you the ropes."

They all laughed. Melanie's eyes felt moist as she looked at the beaming faces of her closest friends. "You guys are too much. This is really nice of you"

"That's us," Coren said. "Nice, nice, nice. Now sit down and start opening your presents!"

Melanie began with a large box tagged BIG SISTER SURVIVAL KIT. Inside she found hairbrushes. "Because she'll always be borrowing yours," Coren explained. "Trust me on this."

Next, Melanie unwrapped a spray bottle of insect repellent. "Just in case the kid becomes a pest like my brother," Mindy joked.

Digging deeper, Melanie found a sign that read, KEEP OUT. TRESPASSERS WILL BE SHOT and another that read, SIBLING RIVALRY—OPPOSITES ATTACK. Then she unwrapped a bag of candy—for bribing kid brothers and sisters into getting lost. At the bottom of the box was a scrapbook with her friends' pictures in it, free coupons to redeem for babysitting, and spaces for filling out statistics on her soon-to-be sibling.

"Look at this," Justine said. She unfolded a large poster of a family tree. "You fill in all the blanks with the names of your relatives. It's kind of fun. I did one in health class last year and thought you might like to do one, too."

Coren leaned toward her. "You might not want to write in Freddy Krueger's name. Sometimes it's okay not to include *everybody* in the family."

Melanie made a face at the joke. Then, shoving aside the torn wrapping paper, she

aid, "This is too sweet. Thanks. Really. It
neans so much to me."

"Can you call us when your mom goes
nto labor?" Mindy asked. "Maybe we
ould all come to the hospital and wait with
ou."

"Mom's going to a special birthing room,
nd a midwife is going to help her deliver the
aby. Dad's coaching her," Melanie ex-
lained. "I won't see the actual birth, but
here's a big waiting room. I guess you all
ould come down and wait with me."

"What if it's born in the middle of the
ight?" Anna asked.

"We're all out of school. What would it
natter?" Coren said. "Call me anytime, day
r night."

"Me too," Justine said. "I'll pick everyone
p." She was the oldest of the group and
lready had her driver's license.

"It could be fun," Melanie said. "Like a
leepover."

"I'll bring cookies," Mindy said

"Sodas," Lorna volunteered.

"Jigsaw puzzles and board games," Faith
aid "My aunt took twelve hours to have
er baby "

"My mom told me I came in three hours," Melanie said. "Maybe this baby will be in a hurry to get born, too."

The group applauded.

Melanie raised her can of soda. "A toast. To us. To my mom and dad. To a Christmas baby and a short labor."

The group of friends raised their soda cans high and clinked them together. Melanie couldn't have been happier. This was going to be the best Christmas of her life.

Three

"Mellie. Wake up. It's time."

Melanie heard her father's voice as if from far away. She struggled through layers of sleep, forced her eyes open, and saw him in the doorway of her bedroom, lit from behind by the light in the hall. She bolted upright. "Time for what? What time is it?"

"It's one in the morning. We're headed to the hospital. Your mom's in labor."

"I'm up," she said. Melanie scrambled out of bed. She reached for socks, jeans, sweater, and jacket, her heart pounding in expectation. "Where's Mom?"

"She's downstairs waiting while I war
up the car," her father answered as he hu
ried toward the stairs.

Melanie grabbed the backpack she ha
filled days before with makeup, a tootl
brush, a small pillow, phone numbers, snac
food, and books, and clambered downstair

She found her mother sitting in the livin
room, gazing at the Christmas tree ablaz
with lights. "Well, I didn't make it to Chris
mas Day. Are you disappointed?"

"No way." Melanie knelt beside he
mother's chair. "This is great." She tried t
remember the date.

"The twentieth," her mother said, as
reading her mind.

"So we'll be home in time for Christma
We'll open all our presents and eat a bi
turkey dinner. And the baby will be tucke
in the new nursery. It'll be super." Just th
day before, Melanie had placed a mound c
packages for the baby beneath the tree. O
every tag she'd written, FOR BABY MORTIME
MORTICIA, FROM SANTA. "This way, I ca
change the tags to the baby's real name," sh
added brightly.

Her mother stiffened and took several deep breaths.

"Are you okay? Does it hurt?" Melanie wished her father would hurry.

"It's just labor. No pain, no gain." She took Melanie's hand and placed it on her round belly.

"It feels like a rock."

"The muscles are doing their job. They have to force the baby down and out."

"It's got to hurt."

Her mother laughed. "It's normal, Mellie. And it's only just started. It could be a long night."

"I have stuff to do." Melanie patted her backpack. "Some of my friends want to come and wait with me. We'll have a little party."

"Don't get too noisy. I may not be the only woman in labor tonight."

"You'll be the most important one, though," Melanie declared.

Just then, her father came in from the garage. "Your chariot's warm and ready to roll, Cinderella." He helped his wife to her feet. "Are you sure you're ready for this?"

"Too late to back out now," Connie joked. He kissed her forehead and led her toward the car. "Unplug the tree lights, Mellie."

Melanie hurried, pausing only long enough to glance up at the star atop the tree. "Here we go," she whispered. "Keep on shining."

As they drove to the hospital, Melanie timed her mother's contractions. When they arrived, her mother was placed in a wheelchair and rolled into a birthing room. Melanie had come with her parents during their orientation tour, so she knew the general layout of the facility. She'd also met the midwife, Vera, who would do the delivery.

Her mother's room contained a hospital bed, a sofa, a TV, a couple of chairs, a private bathroom, and a window that looked out onto the night sky. Vera helped Melanie's mom into bed and started an IV solution. "For hydration," she explained, then added, "I need to do an exam to see how far along you are, Connie." She asked Melanie and her dad to leave for a few minutes.

Outside in the hall, it was eerily quiet.

Lights were dim, and Melanie felt as if they were the only two people awake in the world.

"Excited?" her dad asked.

"Oh, Daddy. It's so wonderful. How about you?"

He put his arm around her shoulder. "I never thought I'd be a new father again. I figured I'd be standing around with *your* husband, waiting for *your* baby to be born instead of mine."

"Does this mean I can start dating?"

He laughed. "Not yet. You're still my little girl."

Melanie poked him in the side. "Your big girl now. Do you care whether it's a boy or a girl?" Her mother had told her it didn't matter.

"In my opinion, we've done 'girl' pretty well already. You'll be a hard act to follow. But, no, I don't care."

She smiled. Sometimes her dad made her feel wonderful. "Did Mom tell you that we want to name her Jennifer Lorraine if it's a girl?"

"She did. And I think my mother would be proud to have a namesake."

"And if it's a boy, we've picked Matthe
Tyler . . . after Mom's maiden name."

"I approve of both choices."

Vera opened the door. "You can go
now. She's got a ways to go, but everythir
is looking good."

In the room, Melanie's mother was cast
ally flipping through TV channels. "N
much on in the middle of the night," sl
said, clicking off the remote.

"Aren't you hurting?" Melanie aske
thinking that her mother looked prett
bored.

"It comes and goes," her mother sai
"The labor pains are about seven minute
apart now." She tensed. "Here comes on
now, Frank."

Melanie's father took his wife's hand an
spoke to her encouragingly while she too
short, panting breaths as she'd been taugl
in Lamaze class. When the contractio
passed, she sank into the pillow.

Seeing her mother in pain was difficult f
Melanie, so she excused herself and wer
down the hall to an empty waiting roon
From there she called Justine, staked
claim on a couple of tables, and sat down t

wait Within an hour, Justine arrived with several friends.

"This is so cool," Coren said. Faith and Mindy plopped on nearby sofas with pillows they'd brought, while Justine laid out a tray of cookies and sodas.

Melanie returned to her mother's room frequently to check on her progress, then reported back to the group. By four in the morning, everyone but she and Coren had fallen asleep. They played double solitaire and watched the clock.

"How's it going?" Coren asked the moment Melanie returned from her latest tour down the hall.

"They gave Mom some pain medication, so she's resting between contractions. The midwife said it won't be long now."

"Too bad you have to miss the big moment."

"I tried to talk Mom and Dad into letting me watch, but they said no. I'm going to wait out in the hall, though, with my ear to the door. Dad's promised to yell out 'girl' or 'boy' the second the baby's born."

"Then can you see it?"

"Once the baby's cleaned up and Mom's

taken care of, I can go inside." Melanie looked up at the clock. "This is taking forever."

Suddenly her father hurried into the room. He was wearing a green paper gown and looked excited. "Come on, Mellie. The baby's almost here."

She jumped up and ran after him, then skidded to a stop outside the door. He'd left it open just enough for her to hear Vera barking orders to a nurse and telling Melanie's father where to stand. Coren and the other girls straggled sleepily down the hall and clustered around the door with Melanie.

Melanie heard Vera say, "This is it, Connie. Push hard. I can see the top of the baby's head."

Melanie held her breath. Next she heard a wail and the midwife announcing, "It's a girl!"

Tears of joy filled Melanie's eyes. A sister. She had a sister. Her friends gave out muffled squeals and hugged her.

Then she heard her father say, "Where are you going? Why are you taking her away? I thought we could hold her."

Her mother called, "Frank? What's happening? I want to see our baby."

The midwife's voice replied, "I'm just taking her to the doctor so she can have a quick look at her. I'll be right back. Calm down. Don't worry."

Melanie's heart froze. Something was wrong with her brand-new baby sister.

Four

Melanie pushed open the door and ran into the room. "Mom, Dad . . . what's happening?"

"We don't know." Her father stroked her mother's forehead. She was crying and clinging to his hand.

A nurse injected some medication into her IV line with a syringe. "This will help you rest," she said.

"I don't want to rest. I want my baby," Melanie's mother wailed, but in moments, she was out.

Melanie saw bloody sheets and felt woozy. Her father gently slipped his arm around her. The nurse turned to Melanie's father. "I have to attend to your wife right now. Please step out into the hall."

"I have questions." His voice sounded un steady.

"In a minute," the nurse said firmly. "Your wife comes first."

Melanie and her dad went into the corridor, where her friends stood huddled together. "What's wrong?" Coren asked.

"We don't know anything. They took the baby away."

"Please, girls, you'd better go on home," her father told the group. "Mellie will call you as soon as she can, as soon as we know something more."

Quietly they slipped away, looking over their shoulders, their eyes wide, their gazes anxious.

When the nurse allowed Melanie and her dad back into the room, Melanie's mother was dressed in a clean gown and sleeping on fresh bed linen. Melanie's father took the nurse's elbow and said, "For the love of heaven, tell me what's going on!"

"Mr. Barton, don't be alarmed—"

"Are you serious? Of course I'm alarmed.

Everything goes fine, the baby is born, then the midwife snatches her away saying the doctor has to see her. I want to talk to someone, and I mean right now!"

"I'll get the doctor," the nurse said, leaving the room.

Melanie threw herself into her father's arms. "Oh, Daddy. There's something horrible going on with my sister, isn't there?"

"I don't know. I barely caught a glimpse of her. I'll get to the bottom of this, honey, and when your mother wakes up, she'll have her baby to hold."

"Jennifer," Melanie said in a small voice. "Remember . . . her name is Jennifer."

"Yes," he whispered. "My daughter Jennifer."

"I'm calling in Dr. Singh for a consultation. He'll run some tests and then we'll know what we're dealing with." The woman who spoke to Melanie and her father in the cubicle-size room had introduced herself as Dr. Morrison, a pediatrician on call for the night.

"But something is wrong with the baby,

isn't it?" Melanie's father leaned closer to the doctor, his face grim.

Beside him, Melanie sat stiffly, her hands clasped to keep them from trembling. She felt cold and numb.

"It seems so. Yes." The doctor's words hit Melanie like blows.

Her father sagged in his chair. "What do you suspect?"

"It's best not to deal in speculation at this point."

"What am I supposed to say to my wife when she wakes up?"

"She's been given a sedative that will make her sleep for at least five or six hours. I suggest that you and your daughter go home, get some rest, and come back later in the day. By then, maybe we'll have some answers."

"I don't want to go home," Melanie blurted out.

The doctor looked at her kindly. "Please. It's been a long night and you're going to need your strength. Your mother's sleeping and so is the baby. There's nothing you can do here."

'Where is Jennifer?" Melanie's father asked.

"In the neonatal ICU "

Melanie's heart thudded as she realized the baby had been placed in the intensive care unit "Can't we even see her?"

"Come with me." Dr. Morrison led them down the hall. She rounded a corner and stopped in front of a thick, plate-glass window. "The babies are in temperature-controlled incubators," she explained.

Melanie stared into a dimly lit, high-tech room where clear plastic incubators held the tiniest of babies. All were hooked to blinking monitors with wires and tubes that hung from their bodies like puppet strings attached to motionless dolls. They wore only paper diapers and little knitted caps. "Why are they all wearing hats?" Melanie asked.

"Babies lose a lot of body heat through their heads, so we keep their heads covered to retain warmth. Some of them have no body fat, and they need the extra insulation," Dr. Morrison explained.

Two nurses worked in the unit. Melanie watched as one nurse checked monitors and

he other sat in a rocking chair, feeding a
baby from a bottle. "What's wrong with
hem?"

"Most are preemies—born before their
ime. One was born with a serious heart de-
ect, and another with Down Syndrome."

"Where's Jennifer?" Melanie's gaze
swept the room

"Over there, in the incubator near the far
wall."

Melanie craned her neck She could
barely make out a mound wrapped in a baby
blanket with a knitted hat on its head "Can't
we see her closer up?"

"Later," Dr. Morrison said. "Please.'

Melanie's father cleared his throat. "Al
right, we'll go home now, but we'll be back
after we get a little sleep And tell this Dr
Singh I'll want some answers."

As Melanie and her father turned a corner, they saw another plate-glass window.
Like a moth to a flame, Melanie was drawn
over, and she looked inside. This room was
brightly lit and the babies lay in rows of incubators. All these infants were tightly
wrapped in blankets and also wore knitted
caps. Some were crying; others lay fast

asleep, oblivious to the noise. These were the normal babies, the healthy ones.

A lump the size of a fist stuck in Melanie's throat. This was where Jennifer should be . . . not in that other room. Not in the room reserved for babies held together by tubes, wires, and technology.

"I'm going to look in on your mother," her father said. His voice sounded thick and scratchy. "They've moved her to a private room."

"I'll wait here," Melanie said.

"Maybe you shouldn't—"

"It's all right, Dad. Go see Mom and then come back for me." She continued to stare at the babies. She counted fourteen, all of them perfectly fine.

A young couple came up alongside her. "There he is, hon," the man said. "In the second row, third from the left."

The woman wore a robe and her hair looked unkempt, but her face fairly glowed. "Isn't he beautiful? Oh, Jerry, he's just fantastic." They nestled against each other. Melanie felt tears stinging her eyes. "Which one's yours?" the woman asked.

Melanie swallowed the lump in her throat.

'My sister's in the other room. There . . . there was a problem."

The couple recoiled, making Melanie feel that they were afraid to get too near her. As if her sister's "problem" might somehow rub off on their happiness. "I'm so sorry," the woman said.

"Me too." Melanie's lips moved woodenly. When her father returned, she walked outside with him. The air felt brittle, like a sheet of thin ice. The sky was pitch black, as if all the stars had gone out. Melanie's teeth chattered. In the car, with the heater going full blast, she asked, "How's Mom?"

"Sound asleep." He ran a hand through his rumpled hair and over his unshaven face. "I put your backpack in her room."

Until that moment, Melanie had forgotten about it. "Thanks."

"I figure we should sleep until nine or so, clean up, and come back. That okay with you?"

"Fine."

"Whatever is wrong with the baby, the doctors will probably be able to fix it," he said. "Medical science can work miracles these days."

His words brought Melanie a ray of hop
He was right. She'd seen stories on T
about amazing surgeries and other astoun
ing procedures. "Do you think the docto
can help Jennifer? She's so tiny."

"They're helping all those preemies. Y
saw it with your own eyes."

"Maybe you're right," Melanie said, fee
ing her spirits lift.

"We've got to think positive," her fathe
said. "We've got to hold on to hope. W
don't know anything yet. Her problem migl
be very fixable."

Melanie reached over and her father too
her hand and squeezed. "You're right," sl
said. "I mean, after all, it's almost Christma
Nothing bad can happen at Christmas."

Her father managed a smile. "That's m
girl."

Melanie stared out the window, blinke
back tears, and told herself again and agai
Nothing bad can happen at Christmas.

Five

It seemed to Melanie as if she'd just lain down when her alarm clock went off. Surprised that she'd even fallen asleep, and still groggy, she stumbled into the bathroom and took a shower. After dressing, she went downstairs to find her father in the kitchen, drinking coffee. He had showered and shaved but still looked exhausted. "I just talked to the nurses and your mother's still asleep. Even so, I'd like to get down there as soon as possible. We'll grab something to eat on the way."

Melanie nodded. "I'm ready when you are. How's Jennifer?"

"She's holding her own."

"What if she—" Melanie stopped, unable to express her greatest fear.

"Let's go," her father said.

Outside, sunlight streamed down and the sky was clear and crystal blue. During the drive back to the hospital, Melanie watched people rush along the sidewalks and past store windows. The sights and sounds that had excited her only days before, now depressed her horribly. How could everybody be happy when her whole world was falling apart? How could she think about Christmas when she didn't know what was wrong with her brand-new baby sister?

At the hospital, she and her father went straight to her mother's room. Her mother was just waking. After hugging her, Melanie excused herself, knowing her parents would want to talk privately.

She went immediately to the neonatal ICU and anxiously looked through the glass window for Jennifer. When Melanie located her incubator, she saw that her sister was hooked to IVs and a heart monitor. Her tiny fists were clenched, as if she were holding on for dear life. "Hang in there, Jennifer," Melnie whispered under her breath. "The doctors will fix you."

Melanie returned to her mother's room to find her sitting up in bed, her eyes red and puffy. "Your father went to the nurses' station," her mother said. "Evidently, Dr. Singh left instructions that he was to be called as soon as I woke up."

"They haven't told you anything?"

Her mother shook her head. "I still feel groggy. Hand me that water pitcher, please."

Melanie watched her mother scoop out a handful of ice chips and wrap them in a washcloth, then press the cloth to her eyes and cheeks. "How do you feel, Mom?"

"Awful." Her mother's voice quavered. "This was supposed to be a happy day, Melie. A happy day."

Melanie wanted to throw herself into her mother's arms and cry, but realized she had to act strong for her mother's sake. "Jennifer looks all right," she offered, attempting to sound encouraging. "I saw her through the window and she looks like she's sleeping. She's pretty, Mom."

The door opened and Melanie's father walked in. "The doctor's on his way." As his

wife got out of bed, he asked, "Should yc
be up?"

"I'm sore, but I'm fine. I want to go an
see my baby as soon as the doctor leaves.'

Melanie's father had just settled h
mother in a chair when they heard a rap c
the door. A short, brown-skinned man wit
dark eyes and black hair, wearing a whi'
lab coat, came in and introduced himself :
Dr. Singh. "I'm a neurologist, and I've bee
called in to consult on your daughter's case

"A neurologist!" Frank Barton sai
sounding confused. "But why?"

Dr. Singh looked at Melanie and sh
stepped closer to her mother's side. She eye
him defiantly. There was no way she wa
going to leave the room. "I do not have goo
news," the doctor said with a slight accen
"And there is no gentle way to tell you this.

Melanie's blood ran cold with his word
She saw her mother grip her father's hand

"Tell us," Connie said.

"Your baby has been born anencephalic.

"Meaning?" Frank asked.

"Meaning that she lacks a fully develope
brain. I've done a CT scan, and your baby i
missing all of her cerebral cortex."

Melanie couldn't quite absorb what the doctor was telling them, but she heard her mother cry out and her father gasp.

Dr. Singh reached into his lab-coat pocket and took out a drawing of the human brain. "The brain consists of three sections," he said, pointing to each area. "The cerebral cortex, the cerebellum, and the brain stem. Jennifer has only these bottom two portions. Her upper brain never formed. Instead, there's only a fluid-filled sac."

"Will she be retarded?" Connie asked.

The doctor's face filled with sympathy. "It means that she has no consciousness, no ability to think or reason."

"But she's alive," Connie blurted out. "She is . . . isn't she?"

"At the moment, yes, but infants with this kind of birth defect do not survive. I'm sorry." Although Melanie could barely see his face through her tears, Dr. Singh looked genuinely sad. "Frankly, it's remarkable she's lived this long. These infants usually die at birth. Maybe two thousand are born each year in this country. We don't know why their upper brains don't develop in the womb, but they don't. Their brain stems are usually intact, as is your baby's, so their nervous systems can function for a time. Their hearts beat and they can breathe, but they can't see, or hear, or respond."

"Neither could Helen Keller." The words were out of Melanie's mouth before she realized it. He couldn't give up on Jennifer. She wouldn't let him!

"Helen Keller had high intelligence. Her handicaps were imposed by illness, not by a birth defect," the doctor said kindly. "Jennifer has no capacity for intelligence."

"What could I have done to cause this?" Melanie's mother cried.

The doctor shook his head. "You did nothing wrong, Mrs. Barton, believe me. These things are often picked up by ultrasound, but in your case, it wasn't. Most parents who know in advance that they're carrying anencephalic babies choose to abort them."

Melanie saw her parents cringe. "We would not have done that," her mother whispered. "Regardless of whether or not we had known."

"Then it does not matter," Dr. Singh said.

"Isn't there anything you can do for her?" Melanie's father asked, distraught.

"All we can do is keep her warm and fed."

"How much time does she have?"

"Possibly a few days. Longer if we put her on a respirator."

"You're certain?"

"I have been a physician for twenty-one years. I have seen six such cases of anencephalic babies. Three were aborted. Two were stillborn. The one that survived lasted but a week."

Melanie's mother stood, swaying slightly. "She's our daughter. We want to see her."

Dr. Singh nodded. "Of course."

As she followed her parents and the doctor down the hall to the neonatal nursery, Melanie felt caught in a nightmare. Surely she'd soon wake up and discover all this had been a bad dream.

Dr. Singh took them behind the nurses' station and into a small room. There he directed them to put on sterile gowns and then led them into the neonatal ICU. Christmas music that had filled the corridors faded, replaced by the constant beeping of electronic monitors.

The doctor stopped beside Jennifer's incubator and Melanie's family gathered around it. Melanie stared down at her tiny sister. Jennifer's chest rose and fell rapidly. The round pads for the lead wires attached to her chest looked huge and dark against her pale skin. On the monitor screen, her heartbeat was etched by a green line.

"Hello, Jennifer," Melanie heard her mother whisper. "How are you, my little one?"

"We're right here with you, baby girl," her father said.

Melanie couldn't speak around the lump in her throat.

"How much does she weigh?" she heard her mother ask.

"Six pounds, two ounces. And she's nineteen inches long."

"Our Melanie was eight and a half pounds."

Melanie couldn't grasp her mother's words. How could she have ever been so little, so delicate and fair?

"Can we hold her?" her mother asked.

Dr. Singh opened the incubator, took a flannel blanket, and wrapped it around the unresponsive infant. He placed her in her mother's arms, careful not to tangle the wires.

Connie cuddled the baby against her chest. Frank traced his finger down the baby's cheek. Against Jennifer's tiny features, his finger looked as if it were attached to a giant's hand. *Maybe the doctors are wrong,* Melanie thought. How could any human being who looked normal be so damaged?

Melanie wanted to hold her, but she was terrified. What if Jennifer stopped breathing in her arms? The knitted hat slipped backward and Melanie recoiled. Beneath the hat was a large, swollen mound of a head covered with fine brown hair. Jennifer's head was misshapen, like an overfilled water balloon, and until now, hidden by the hat. Instantly sick to her stomach, Melanie rushed out of the room. Her sister wasn't normal at all. She was a freak.

Six

"Are you okay?" Melanie's father was bending over her as she lay on a sofa in the lounge. A nurse was taking her blood pressure.

"What happened?" Melanie asked. She felt light-headed.

"You fainted," the nurse said, "but I caught you before you hit the floor."

Melanie struggled to sit up, but her father and the nurse both insisted she stay put. "I— I felt a little sick in there. I just got a little woozy, but I'm all right now. Honest."

"You didn't get much rest," her father said. "I'm sure you're just wiped out."

"This has taken a toll on all of us," her mother said. She was leaning on Dr. Singh's arm and looking anxious. "I don't want anything to happen to you, Mellie."

Grateful that neither of her parents said what the three of them knew was true—that the sight of Jennifer's deformed head had been too much for her—Melanie said, "I'm sorry." She felt ashamed.

A nurse pushed a wheelchair up behind Melanie's mother. "Please, Mrs. Barton, you should be back in your room in bed."

"I'll take her," Frank said.

"No, stay with Melanie."

"I'll go with you," Melanie insisted, sitting upright. "I feel fine now."

Her mother looked up at Dr. Singh from the wheelchair. "Thank you for letting me hold my baby. It meant a lot to finally touch her."

"Your family may be with her anytime. I have told the nurses to allow you admittance. It will be good for all of you."

Once her mother was settled in her bed and given medication to make her sleep, Melanie drove back home with her father. "Is Jennifer really going to die, Dad?"

"That's what the doctor said."

His answer broke her heart. "It's not fair. She's just a little baby."

"You're right—it isn't fair. But there's nothing we can do about it." He cleared his throat. "Listen, I want to be with your mother when she wakes up."

"I want to go with you."

"No. I want you home, resting. You can come later." His refusal was firm and left no room for argument.

At the house, Coren and Justine were sitting on the front porch, huddled in sweaters, coats, and mittens. They jumped up and ran to the car before Melanie's father had even turned off the engine. "What's happening?" Coren asked. "We haven't heard from you."

"I have to return to the hospital and I want Mellie in bed," her father told them.

"Dad, please. Let me talk to my friends."

"We won't stay long, Mr. Barton," Justine promised.

Her dad agreed and drove off. Melanie led her friends inside and plopped down with them on the living room sofa. "It's awful," she said on the verge of tears.

"Tell us everything," Coren said.

As Melanie spoke, they began to cry, too. Coren found her voice first. "No brain? I—I can't believe it."

"Well, I didn't make it up."

"And so she's just going to *die*?" Justine looked incredulous.

Melanie didn't trust her voice, so the three girls sat in strained silence. Melanie stared gloomily at the Christmas tree. Had it only been hours since she and her mother had sat in this very room with the soft light shining, the scent of pine all around them, planning for the birth of the baby? It seemed like a lifetime ago. Now the tree looked garish and fake, the heaps of presents gaudy. She saw the pile marked for Baby Mortimer/Morticia and cringed. How stupid of her to have wrapped and tagged them until she knew for certain there would even be a baby. She jumped to her feet.

"Mom doesn't need to come home and see all this stuff," she said. "Help me carry it up and put it in my closet."

Justine and Coren scrambled to pick up the packages.

Melanie headed up to her room, opened her closet, and asked her friends to dump the gaily wrapped gifts on the floor. She shut the door firmly.

"Do you want us to leave?" Coren asked.

Melanie shook her head. "No." She didn't want to be alone. She knew she couldn't sleep, no matter how much her parents wanted her to.

"Want a soda?" Justine asked.

"Okay. There are cans in the fridge. Why don't you get us all one?"

"Back in a flash." Justine ran out.

Melanie began to pace around her room. "Why did this happen to us?" Suddenly angry, she slammed her fist into the bed pillow. "Why my sister? Do you know how long I've wished for a sister?"

"You're like a sister to me," Coren said, a plaintive tone in her voice.

"But Jennifer's my really and truly sister. If you could see her little face. I—I . . ." Her voice broke. Coren came closer, but Melanie waved her aside. "It's Christmas, Coren. Now every Christmas for the rest of my life, I'll remember this horrible, horrible Christmas. What was God *thinking*? Doesn't he know how much this baby meant to us?"

Coren didn't reply. Melanie realized there were no answers to her questions.

Abruptly, she left her room and went to the nursery that stood ready and waiting for the baby who would never come home. Sunlight streamed through the pretty curtains her mother had made for the room. Rows of stuffed animals stretched across the dresser top. Melanie had lined them up like fluffy sentinels to watch over a baby who would not see them. She toyed with the mobile hanging over the crib. The stars and moons twisted, then hung limp. "Mom played classical music for Jennifer every day," Melanie said, her voice breaking. "And she never heard a note." Melanie felt as if the walls were closing in, as if she were suffocating. She wanted to scream and kick and run away. Instead, she stood stock-still, unable to move.

Justine came into the room, carrying cans of soda. "Maybe you shouldn't torture yourself by being in here."

"Come on." Coren took Melanie's hand and led her back to her own room.

She lay on her bed and sobbed. She wept

for the baby, for her parents, for herself. I
nally, when she was all cried out, she fell in
an exhausted sleep.

Melanie awoke with a start and sat u
right, disoriented. Lamps were on in h
room. Outside the window, gray Decemb
dusk had fallen. Coren and Justine we
lounging on the floor, reading magazines,
deck of cards spread out on the carpe
"What time is it?" Melanie asked.

"Five o'clock," Coren said.

"You stayed all afternoon while I slept?

"Of course. We weren't about to go c
and leave you."

Touched, Melanie said, "Thanks. I hop
you weren't too bored."

"You snore," Justine said with an encou
aging smile.

Melanie made a face at her and the thr
of them laughed. For Melanie, the laught
felt good. She couldn't recall the last tin
she'd smiled. "Is my dad home?" She slid o
the bed.

"Not yet."

"I want to go back to the hospital." Me
anie felt a sudden urgency. She didn't wa

anything to happen to Jennifer while she wasn't there, and Dr. Singh had said that the baby wouldn't live long.

"I'll drive us," Justine said.

At her bedroom door, Melanie stopped. "Just a minute. There's something I have to get." She rummaged through the stack of discarded gifts in her closet until she found what she was looking for.

"What is it?" Coren asked.

"Something I want Jennifer to have," Melanie said. "I owe it to her."

Tucking the box under her arm, she grabbed her coat. In minutes she, Coren, and Justine were headed for the hospital.

Melanie went straight to the neonatal ICU, her friends following along. Her heart pounded as she looked through the window for Jennifer's incubator. She felt a wave of relief when she saw it on the far side of the room. "There she is."

Coren and Justine craned their necks. "Wow, she's tiny," Coren said.

"Wait here."

Melanie gowned up and slipped into the ICU. She saw Coren and Justine wave to her from the other side of the glass, and she felt like a fish inside an aquarium. Trembling, she approached Jennifer's incubator. The only signs of life were her rising and falling chest and the green squiggly line of her heartbeat on the monitor.

"It's me, Jennifer . . . your sister, Melanie. I'm sorry about the way I acted earlier. I really am." Melanie knew that Jennifer couldn't hear her, but still she had to say the words. "I hope you'll forgive me. Not enough sleep, I guess." She held up the box. "I have a Christmas present for you. I bought it before you were born. Before we even knew who you were. I thought I'd give it to you now."

Seven

"C an I help you?"

The nurse's voice startled Melanie.

I—I want to give my sister a present."

The nurse smiled and Melanie saw sympathy on her face. "That'll be fine. Let me help." She opened the incubator.

Melanie tore the wrapping paper off the box and pulled out a long red Santa stocking hat with a white fluffy ball on the end. On the snowy white brim was stitched "#1 Elf" in bright green letters. "Can I put it on her?"

"Certainly."

Gingerly, with trembling fingers, Melanie touched Jennifer's head. She took a deep

breath and eased off the knitted cap. Th
time, Jennifer's head did not seem so di
torted and misshapen. Melanie stroked th
baby's downy light-brown hair.

"Go ahead," the nurse urged.

Melanie stretched the stocking hat ov
the baby's head, pulling it down onto he
forehead so the words showed. Tears poole
in her eyes.

"She looks adorable," the nurse sai
"How thoughtful of you."

"But she doesn't know, does she? She
never know."

The nurse closed the incubator. "Not i
the conventional way," she answered. "B
perhaps she knows in another way. In th
way people just sense things sometimes. Lik
you sense that someone's about to say som
thing, and then they do. Or the phone
about to ring, and it does. Did you ever hav
that happen?"

Melanie nodded, appreciative of th
nurse's kindness. She glanced around at th
sleeping babies. A sense of foreboding cam
over her. "How are the others?"

"Actually, they're all doing well. Excep

for the little guy over there." The nurse pointed to a baby who was partially obscured by numerous wires and tubes. "He has a defective heart."

Melanie remembered being told about him earlier. "Can't the doctors fix it?"

"Afraid not. He needs a heart transplant, but there's a real shortage of infant donor hearts, so it's unlikely he'll get one."

"Then he'll die, just like Jennifer." Melanie was resigned to her sister's fate. Still, the words tasted bitter.

The nurse sighed. "I wish we could save them all, but we can't. Sometimes all we can do is keep them warm and fed and make them comfortable."

"Well, thank you for taking care of my sister."

The nurse smiled. "Thank you for saying so."

Coren was wiping her eyes with a tissue when Melanie came out of the ICU. "I remember the day we bought that hat at the mall. You were going to take her picture in it on Christmas morning."

"Plans change," Melanie said sadly.

"Look, I'm staying to see my mom, but there's no need for you two to hang around this place anymore. When you talk to the others, tell them what's going on, but ask them not to come down here, okay?" Melanie couldn't stand the thought of everyone rushing to the hospital to stare at her dying sister. Jennifer—all these babies—should be left in peace.

"We'll pass on your message," Justine said.

Coren squeezed Melanie's hand. "I guess we'll see you later."

"Sure. Later. Probably after Christmas." Christmas was four days away. By then, her sister most likely would be dead. Melanie forced a tight smile and said goodbye to her friends.

Melanie walked into her mother's room to find her parents praying with Pastor Hitchings. Her mother looked up. Tears streaked her face. "Oh, Mellie, I'm glad you're here.'

"Coren and Justine brought me. I—I couldn't stay away. What's going on?"

Her father slipped his arm around her

shoulders. "We want to have Jennifer baptized."

Melanie glanced from her parents into the kind, sympathetic eyes of the young pastor. "Why did God let this happen? He could have stopped it, you know. He's *God*."

"We may never know why this side of heaven," the pastor said. "We just have to trust in him."

"Why should I?" Melanie answered angrily. "If he lets this happen to a little baby—"

"Mellie!" her mother interrupted her. "Don't be disrespectful."

"It's all right," Pastor Hitchings said. "Your daughter has every reason to ask why." He turned back to Melanie. "I've spent years of my life studying God. Learning about him and getting to know him. And I've come to believe that one of the things I owe God is my trust. Just like when your parents kept you from chasing your ball out into a busy street when you were little. I'll bet it made no sense at all when they yelled at you to stop just before you stepped off the curb. Why were they yelling? All you wanted was to get your ball. But they knew about cars racing down streets, and how dangerous it was. Years later, you understand about cars too, but at the time it made no sense.

"None of us can grasp God's purpose now for Jennifer's condition. And truthfully, we may never understand. But I do know enough about God's character to know that what he does, he does for our good, and I must trust him no matter how sad or bad I feel, or how unfair I think things are."

Melanie conceded his point, but she still felt angry.

"We'll see her again someday," Connie said, clutching her husband's hand. "When we're all in heaven together."

Melanie believed that was true, but she wanted Jennifer to be with them now. She recalled her dreams about having a sister—cuddling her, taking her for walks, and playing in the park. Shattered dreams.

"Let's go to the ICU," Melanie's father said, interrupting her thoughts.

They walked down the hall, Melanie and her father supporting Connie's arms, with Pastor Hitchings close behind. "The doctor's letting me go home tomorrow," Connie said. "I don't want to be around here anymore. It's too sad for me."

Inside the ICU, the four of them went to Jennifer's incubator. She lay just as Melanie had left her, the Santa Elf hat covering her head. "I—I wanted her to have the hat," Melanie explained.

Connie smiled. "It's precious. We'll take a picture so that we can always remember her."

Melanie's father lifted Jennifer and laid her in Connie's arms. "Hi, little one," Connie said. "We're here with you. All of us . . . Mom, Dad, your big sister. And we all love you so much." She gently handed the baby to the minister.

Pastor Hitchings took a small vial of water from his pocket, eased the hat off Jennifer's head, and said, "Jennifer Lorraine Barton, child of the covenant promise, I baptize you in the name of the Father, Son, and Holy Spirit." He sprinkled the water atop her oddly shaped head as he spoke. Then he bowed his head and prayed for all of them.

Melanie comforted herself with visions of angels passing Jennifer from one to another.

But when she opened her eyes, she was struck by the harsh reality of the intensely cold room full of high technology.

Back out in the hall, Melanie's father walked with the minister while Melanie and her mother stared through the window at Jennifer. She remembered her Big Sister Kit back home and the family tree chart. She wondered about filling in Jennifer's name and asked her mother.

"Certainly. She exists. It's just that her tree branch won't go any further. You'll be the one to carry on now, Mellie. You and your children. The baby to join our family next will be a grandchild for your father and me."

Melanie hung her head and felt her mother's arms come around her. She laid her head on her mother's shoulder. From down the hall, she heard someone call, "Did you see him?" and another voice say, "He's the cutest baby in the nursery. Congratulations and Merry Christmas."

Tears fell down Melanie's cheeks, soaking into her mother's robe.

*   *   *

Melanie and her father arrived at the hospital the next morning before nine. While Melanie's dad handled the paperwork for his wife's discharge, Melanie and her mom went to see Jennifer.

"Did she have a good night?" her mother asked a nurse who was busy changing the diaper of one of the preemies.

"She's holding her own."

Connie lifted Jennifer's hand and kissed the tiny fingers. "I've got to leave you, Jennifer, but I'll be back soon."

"Me too," Melanie said. She wanted Jennifer's eyes to open and see them. Then she remembered that, without a cerebral cortex, Jennifer would not have been able to see. She was blind and deaf. Maybe God would give sight and hearing to her in heaven.

"This is breaking my heart," her mother said. "We'll come back later."

Melanie followed her to the door, stopped, and looked toward the wall where the baby with the defective heart had been. She saw only an empty incubator. "The baby that was inside," she quietly asked the nurse. "Did you move him?"

"We lost him," the nurse replied. "About two A.M., I think. His little heart gave out."

Back home, Connie insisted that she felt fine physically. She made some phone calls as Melanie helped with chores and did laundry. Melanie's dad went to his office for a few hours, explaining that with the holidays so close he needed to clear his desk. Melanie figured he just needed to get his mind off Jennifer.

She and her mother both avoided the nursery. Later that afternoon, Melanie tried to read a book but couldn't concentrate. She still had presents to wrap, but she had completely lost her Christmas spirit. She was sitting in the kitchen with her mother, drinking warm apple cider, when the phone rang. Her mother answered and immediately her face turned pale. "Yes. Please . . . yes, yes. We'll be right there."

'What's wrong?" Melanie asked as soon as her mother hung up. Her heart pounded crazily.

"That was the hospital. Jennifer's having trouble breathing and they want to put her on a respirator."

Eight

Melanie and her mother took a cab to the hospital, because Connie had been told by her doctors not to drive so soon after the baby's birth. She had called her husband before leaving and he arrived at the hospital at practically the same time. "What's happened?" he asked, after giving his wife and daughter a hug.

"Dr. Singh wanted to put Jennifer on a respirator. I told him yes."

They hurried to the ICU. Dr. Singh met them outside the unit.

"How's my baby?"

"She's resting more comfortably now, Mrs. Barton."

"Thank God."

"We want to see her," Frank said.

Before they could take a step, Dr. Singh put his hand on Connie's shoulder. "Mrs. Barton, you understand this does not change Jennifer's prognosis, don't you? All the respirator is doing is allowing her to breathe more easily, which helps relieve strain on her heart."

Melanie watched the light of hope die in her mother's eyes. "Yes. We understand. For a moment I forgot."

The doctor stepped aside and, after slipping into the sterile gowns, Melanie and her parents went inside the ICU. Jennifer lay in her incubator like a limp doll. A white hose protruded from her mouth, held in place by a crisscross of white tape. The tubing leading to the respirator was crowded next to her heart monitor.

Melanie understood exactly what Dr. Singh had said. Nothing could prevent Jennifer from dying, but they could at least make her more comfortable until the inevitable happened. "Maybe we should take off her hat," she said, suddenly concerned that it looked too frivolous for what was happening.

"No," her father said. "Leave it. You bought it for her. You wanted her to have it. I want her to wear it."

Melanie stood staring down at the baby, watching her chest rise and fall, watching her heartbeat on the monitor, not knowing how to say goodbye to someone who had never even known she existed.

They returned home that night, exhausted. "You both should eat something," Frank told his wife and daughter.

"I'm not hungry," Connie said.

"Me either," Melanie said.

"It doesn't matter. We still have to eat. Life goes on."

He ordered a pizza, and once it arrived, the aroma made Melanie's stomach growl. She realized she hadn't eaten since the morning. After devouring a slice, she felt better, less depressed. Looking across the table at her parents, Melanie thought they looked as if they'd aged years in just these few days. She also realized it was time for

her to say what had been on her mind all d₂
long.

She cleared her throat. "I've been thin₁
ing about something and I was wondering
we could talk about it."

"Of course," her father said without e₁
thusiasm.

Melanie took a deep breath. "You kno₁
that baby with the bad heart who died₁
Her parents nodded. "It doesn't seem righ
does it—that he had a working mind and
bad body part, while Jennifer has a perfe₁
body but no upper brain? Neither of the₁
ever had a chance."

"No, it doesn't seem right," her moth₁
said. "But neither can be fixed."

"Maybe." Melanie picked a mushroom o
her second slice of pizza. "One of the nurs₁
told me that lots of babies could live if the
had an organ transplant. What would yo
think of donating Jennifer's organs to he₁
those babies?"

Neither of her parents said a word. Me
anie was afraid she'd wounded them wit
her suggestion. Finally her father sat bac₁
"I believe in organ donation," he said slowl₁
"In fact, I'm a donor. I checked the box o

my driver's license so that if I was ever brought into a hospital in such bad shape that they couldn't save me, they could harvest my organs."

"When I get my license, I'm checking the box to be an organ donor, too," Melanie said. "It does seem the best thing to do to help others. I just thought that maybe Jennifer could help others . . . like that little boy who died." Melanie looked at her mother expectantly. "How do you feel about this, Mom?"

"I believe in organ donation, too—certainly for me. But I'm not sure about it for Jennifer."

"The nurse in the ICU told me that babies die all the time because there's a shortage of infant donors. It seems like it would be a good thing . . . to give Jennifer's organs to some baby so that it could have a chance of living. Don't you think so?"

Her mother's eyes filled with tears. "I—I don't know."

"It would certainly give meaning to her life," Melanie's father said thoughtfully. "It might bring some kind of meaning to this whole catastrophe."

"How can we just dole her out like that?' Her mother looked upset. "A piece to this one, a part to that one."

"Because someone will benefit," Melanie s father told her, reaching for her hand. "And we might spare some poor parents what we're going through now."

"If it were me hooked to those machines," Melanie said, "I would want you to do it. I wouldn't want to die and be stuck in the ground when a part of me could go to help somebody else live."

"Do you really feel that strongly about it?"

"Yes, Mom, I do. Shouldn't something good come from something terrible, if it's possible?"

"I—I'll have to think about it," her mother said.

"We can discuss it with Dr. Singh, Connie," her father said. "We won't do anything unless all of us are in one hundred percent total agreement, all right? But I believe we should at least discuss the possibility. I know it would make me feel better."

Later, when her mother had gone to bed and Melanie was clearing the table, her fa-her came into the kitchen. "I hope I didn't upset Mom with my suggestion," Melanie said. "Or you."

"I'm all right about it," her father said. "It might take your mom a little while to accept it, but I think she will." He reached out and took Melanie by her shoulders. "It was a very adult suggestion, Mellie."

"It was?"

"Thinking of others when you're hurting inside like we all are . . ." He lifted her chin. "You really are growing up, aren't you?"

His words surprised her. Wasn't this what she'd wanted? To have her dad stop treating her like a child? To recognize that she was almost an adult? Ironically, now that he was acknowledging it, it didn't seem important at all. A lump of emotion swelled in her throat. "You always said I was your little girl. Are you replacing me?"

His tired gaze softened and he smiled. "Think of it as a graduation. From most favored little daughter to most favored grown-up daughter."

Melanie laid her cheek against her father's chest. "I'm right, though, aren't I, Daddy?

Jennifer's life should count for somethin shouldn't it?" She saw it clearly. Although was impossible for Jennifer to live, it needn be impossible for other babies. By giving h organs to others, Jennifer could, in a wa continue to live through them.

"You're right," he answered. "Ever body's life should count, regardless of ho short it may be."

Melanie went to bed that night feelin better than she had since Jennifer's birt And standing at her bedroom window, she gazed up at the stars in the night sky, sh wondered if they were as cold and void life as science surmised. Or were they sp cial places in the vast regions of space whei God housed the souls of his little ones?

Nine

"Your offer is kind, generous, an act of love and understanding. And yes, infant organs are urgently needed all over the country. Over fifteen hundred babies die each year waiting for transplants. But we can't accept Jennifer's organs." The man who spoke, Mr. Lawrence, was head of organ-donation services at the hospital. Dr. Singh had brought him into the private conference room where Melanie and her parents were gathered late the following morning.

For a moment Melanie sat staring at Mr. Lawrence in stunned silence, not positive she'd heard him correctly. At breakfast that morning, she and her parents had talked again about giving permission for Jennifer's organs to be harvested. They were in agreement—it was the only option that made sense in this entire tragedy.

"I lay awake thinking about it all night," her mother had said tearfully. "I know it's the best thing to do."

They had hugged each other, then headed for the hospital. Now they were being told they couldn't do it.

"But why?" Melanie heard her father ask. "There's a need, but we can't help fill it? This is crazy."

Mr. Lawrence leaned forward across the table, his expression both kind and sad. "It's the law, Mr. Barton."

"Perhaps I can help explain it," Dr. Singh offered. "Let's begin with the legal definition of death. A patient must be declared brain dead before he can be taken off a respirator and his organs removed for transplantation—"

"But you've told us that Jennifer has no brain." Connie broke into the doctor's explanation.

"She has no upper brain, but she has a functioning brain stem. Her heart is beating, her blood is circulating . . . until her automatic responses cease, technically, she is alive under the law."

"But she's on a respirator. A machine is breathing for her. And you told us that despite the respirator, her heart will fail."

"Yes, that is true," Dr. Singh said.

"Why can't you use her organs once she dies?" Melanie's father asked, looking baffled and frustrated.

"Because as her organs fail, they begin to deteriorate. Once she dies, her organs also die and therefore are useless for transplantation. Which is also why even if a baby is stillborn, its organs can't be used."

"So you're saying that you would have had to take her organs the moment she was born in order for them to be used for transplants?"

"That is correct. For organs to be viable, a physician would have to expedite the anencephalic baby's death. And that cannot be done."

"How confusing," Melanie's mother said,

her voice flat and emotionless. "I could have aborted her, and that would have been legal. But I can't give permission for you to help her die quickly so that her organs could be used to save another baby. That would be murder." She shook her head in confusion. "It makes no sense to me."

"Nevertheless, that is the law," Dr. Singh said.

Melanie listened carefully, keeping her opinions to herself. She wished she could open the door or a window and breathe fresh air. The air in the room had become stale and heavy, weighted down with words and principles that confused her and felt like lead in her heart.

"Let me add something," Mr. Lawrence said, pressing his fingers together. "It's true that infants such as Jennifer are profoundly compromised by their birth defect, but they are still real live human beings. We can't destroy them, even though it might bring good to another. Where would we draw the line? Who would decide how much damage is appropriate before a person's life could be terminated? The mark of an advanced society is how well it treats its very young, its very old, its sick and handicapped."

Melanie's father raised his hand. "Enough. Please, we understand what you're telling us. We can't donate Jennifer's organs." Frank stood, and so did the others. "Then I guess there's nothing further to discuss."

"Except to say thank you," Mr. Lawrence said. "Not every family is as caring or as thoughtful as yours. Donating one's organs is an act of profound giving. I'm only sorry that in this case, we can't accept the gift you're offering."

"We'd like to see Jennifer now," Connie said, starting for the door.

The group left the room, but in the hall, Melanie's father stopped her. "Did you understand everything that was said, Mellie? It's important that you do. We're a family and we're in this together."

Melanie nodded. "He said that Jennifer's organs can't be used to help others because technically she's still alive. And that even after she dies, her organs can't be used because they're dying right along with her."

"Yes," her father said, shaking his head. "How tragically sad."

What Melanie didn't say was that now it appeared Jennifer's brief existence was for nothing. That her short life was without purpose and had absolutely no meaning at all.

The call from the hospital came at eight o'clock on Christmas Eve. Jennifer's tiny heart was failing. Melanie and her parents hurried to the hospital and the neonatal ICU. Dr. Singh was already there, gowned and waiting.

Inside the unit, Jennifer's incubator had been pushed against a wall along with the machines keeping her alive. Jennifer's chest moved up and down to the rhythm of the respirator, but the heart monitor told a different story. The green line, once steady and predictable, appeared erratic and frenetic. Jennifer's heart seemed to be beating itself to death.

Connie wrung her hands. "She's suffering! Do something!"

"She's in no pain," Dr. Singh said, "I assure you."

"What can we do?" Frank's voice sounded strained.

"Let me turn off the respirator," Dr Singh said. "It's time to let her go."

Melanie saw her parents look deep into each other's eyes. Then her mother turned and looked at her. "Is it all right with you, Mellie?"

Not trusting her voice, Melanie could only nod.

Dr. Singh opened the incubator, then reached over and shut off the respirator. Jennifer's chest rose, fell, rose, fell again, then stopped moving. Seconds later, the green line slowed and went flat. The heart monitor let out a piercing whine. Dr. Singh clicked it off, too.

"Can we hold her?" Connie asked.

Dr. Singh reached in, untaped the respirator hose from the baby's mouth, and pulled it out of her throat. He unhooked her IV line and removed the heart-monitor pads from her chest. He lifted the baby out and laid her in Connie's arms.

Melanie watched her mother nuzzle Jennifer, whisper something to her, then pass her body to Melanie's father. He held Jennifer to his cheek, against the stubble of his beard, and kissed her forehead. He looked at Melanie. "You don't have to hold her if you don't want to."

"I want to." Melanie was beyond feeling. She was numb, her mind blank, her reflexes on automatic pilot. She took the lifeless body of her sister. Jennifer felt almost weightless, as if her skin were made of paper, her bones of sticks. Her skin was already growing cool, her color turning ashen, her lips and fingertips bluish. Melanie wondered what color her eyes might have been. "Goodbye, baby sister," she whispered. "I'll miss you."

Dr. Singh took Jennifer's body. "She was quite lovely," he said. "You should be very proud to have given her life."

Melanie and her parents had turned to leave when he asked, "Do you want her hat?"

Melanie did want it. She would put it with her Big Sister Kit from her friends. She'd store it with the family tree chart, and someday, if she ever had children, she would take it out, show it to them, tell them all about her sister—their aunt—and her brief life.

"Thank you," she said, taking the hat from him.

She rubbed it against her face. It was warm and soft and smelled of Jennifer Lorraine Barton, who had lived only four days, but who had changed the course of all their lives forever.

Ten

Melanie sat in the front pew of the darkened church. Recessed spotlights set high in the rafters cast the stone altar in soft, pale yellow. She stared at the altar, at the rows of poinsettias set across the steps, and at the Christmas tree decorated with Christmonds—symbols of the Christian faith.

Behind the altar, a magnificent stained-glass window rose tall and glowing. In the balcony, the organist was practicing for Christmas morning service. He played "Silent Night," and the familiar words kept running through Melanie's head. "Silent night,

holy night, all is calm, all is bright. . . ."
She forced them away. Inside her heart,
nothing was calm and the world was dark.

On the red carpeted steps leading to the
altar, Melanie saw pieces of straw from
the children's pageant earlier that evening.
The church must have been packed with
families coming to see the Sunday-school
children perform the annual telling of the
Christmas story. When she'd been a child,
she often performed in the play while her
parents sat beaming in the pews. At this moment, she wished with all her heart she could
be a little child again, untouched by sadness
and death.

The music finally ceased and Melanie
heard the organist gathering up his things
and leaving. Alone. She liked it better this
way. She heard the sound of the church door
opening and someone's muffled footsteps
coming down the carpeted aisle.

"Melanie? What are you doing here?"

Surprised, she looked up and saw Coren.
"Jennifer died tonight," she said.

Coren sank into the pew beside her. "Oh,
no. Oh, Mellie, that's so sad. I'm really
sorry."

"She never had a chance, you know"
Melanie twisted a shredded tissue in he
hands. "Anyway, Mom and Dad wanted t
talk to Pastor Hitchings, to make arrange
ments for Jennifer's funeral. He told them t
come by his office tonight. They're talking t
him now. I didn't want to go in with them"
Melanie looked at her friend, realizing that
was late on Christmas Eve and that Core
should be home with her family. "Why ar
you here?"

"My brother left his watch behind th
preacher's podium and Mom was afrai
someone would step on it. He forgot to tak
it off for the pageant. He was an angel." Sh
rolled her eyes. "Talk about miscasting . .
anyway, his teacher noticed it just before h
was to go onstage and suggested that per
haps the angels weren't wearing watche
when they made their big announcement t
the shepherds, so he took it off and put it—
Coren interrupted herself. "I'm sorry, I go
carried away. I didn't mean to."

In spite of her sadness, Melanie smile
and waved aside Coren's apology. "Remem
ber the year I got to be Mary?"

"Yup, and I had to play Herod because w

didn't have enough boys in the class. I was so jealous of you. Mary is the starring role."

"It must have been hard on her . . . on Mary, that is. You know, to go all that way to Bethlehem, and not have reservations anywhere, and to end up having her baby in a stable. No neonatal ICU if anything went wrong." Melanie sighed. "But at least she got to watch her baby grow up."

"Sure, Mary got to watch Jesus grow up, but she had to watch him die, too. Remember? She went to his execution."

"We watched Jennifer die." Fresh tears filled Melanie's eyes.

Coren shook her head. "It's just too sad. Whenever I think about it, all I do is cry." She eased out of the pew. "My dad's waiting in the car. I'd better find that watch and go." She got down on all fours behind the podium, feeling around on the carpet. "Here it is. No one's stepped on it yet." She stopped next to Melanie on her way out. "Will you call me about the funeral? I'd like to come, and I know the others would, too. We don't know what to do or say, but we're your friends, you know."

Melanie nodded. Coren said goodbye,

then hurried away. Again Melanie was alone. Minutes later her parents emerged from the pastor's office and sat beside her, seemingly not in a hurry to leave. Her mother said, "Pastor Hitchings said you could come talk to him if you ever want to."

"What's the point?" Melanie asked. "Talking won't change anything."

"It may make you feel better. I know it made me and your dad feel better."

"Yes, it helped," her father echoed.

"When's the funeral?" Melanie asked.

"On the twenty-seventh. We'll go pick out a casket the day after Christmas."

From an incubator to a casket in four days, Melanie thought. Jennifer had come and gone without ever seeing sunlight, or hearing music, or smelling a Christmas tree. "Four days doesn't seem like much of a life, does it, Mom?"

"Four days," her mother repeated. "Was that all? It seemed like a lifetime."

Melanie shook her head. "Not to me."

"Maybe because I experienced a lifetime of emotion in those four days."

Melanie's father nodded in agreement. "I know I did."

"I still don't get it," Melanie said. "Why was she even born?"

"Why are any of us born?" her father asked.

"I'm glad she was born," her mother said. "I got to hold her and kiss her goodbye. I wouldn't have missed that part for anything. She died in my arms, surrounded by us—her family."

Melanie realized that was true. They'd been together as a family through all of it— her mother's pregnancy, Jennifer's birth, Jennifer's death. Melanie had experienced the cycle of life in a way that took most people seventy or eighty years. She saw, too, that as long as any of them were still alive, Jennifer would be remembered. And the memory of her brief life would always be theirs to share. For they were a *family*. And what remained of their family was different, changed, somehow made bigger, stronger, deeper by Jennifer's existence.

"We should be going," Melanie's father said.

"Yes," her mother said. "I want to go home."

Melanie rose with her parents, and slowly

the three of them walked up the aisle, into the vestibule, and out into the frigid night air. The world lay silent, a thin crust of snow on the church lawn sparkling in the moonlight. "Mom, Dad, we loved her, didn't we?"

"Very much," Connie said.

"More than I ever imagined possible," Frank added.

"Me too," Melanie said. "I'll never forget how much we all loved her. And if she'd never existed, we would never have loved her. We loved her because she belonged to us. To our family."

Melanie stepped between her parents, took their hands, and felt the warmth and comfort of their touch through her gloves. Together the three of them walked to the car, keeping a reverent silence in the starry, starry night.

Book Two

LAST DANCE

One

"Thanks for coming with me. You're a lifesaver."

"It's no big deal," Brenda Scolari assured her friend, Julie. "But I sure wish you could find another place to meet this new dream guy of yours. The hospital isn't exactly the world's most romantic setting, you know."

"True," Julie Hanover said, flinging open her car door and stepping out into the parking lot of the huge Atlanta hospital. "But you've got to admit, coming to visit my uncle is the perfect cover."

Brenda dutifully tagged alongside her friend into the entrance that led to the physical therapy wing, where Julie's uncle was chief of the department. It was also the place where Alan—Julie's heartthrob—worked. Alan was a freshman at nearby Emory University, so Julie rarely got to see him unless she came to the hospital. In Brenda's opinion, as great as her friend Julie was, she was only a high-school junior like herself. So why would Alan care to get involved? He had a college campus full of girls!

"You couldn't find one guy in our high school to like?" Brenda asked. "I mean, you've got nearly a thousand to choose from."

"The same thousand you've looked over," Julie reminded her. "You know all the good ones are taken."

Brenda couldn't argue that point. She'd thought her junior year was going to be spectacular, but her steady boyfriend, Tyler, had moved away over the summer. Now she was right back in the dating game. And pickings were slim.

Julie skidded to a stop in front of her uncle's office and knocked on the door.

"Come on in," his voice called. When they entered, he smiled, put down the file he was reading, and said, "Well, if it isn't my favorite niece and her best friend."

"Hey, Uncle Paul." Julie kissed him on the cheek. "Just stopped by to say hi."

Paul Hanover's eyes twinkled. "This is the third visit in nine days. I can't believe it's me you're really coming to see."

"Of course, it's you," Julie said with wide-eyed innocence.

"You can't fool me. I know there's more to your visits." Paul glanced over at Brenda. "Do you have a crush on somebody here, too?"

Brenda felt her cheeks grow warm. She hated being put on the spot.

"Oh, all right. It's Alan Boyd I'm coming to see," Julie said sheepishly. "But you know Mom wouldn't let me drive across town without a good reason. And when Brenda comes, it's easier to talk Mom into giving me the car keys."

Paul laughed out loud. "You're a sneaky one! But I love you, and I won't tell your secret. Besides, Alan's a fine boy. Now that you're here, go look for him. I think he's finishing a therapy session with Mrs. Wilson." He turned to Brenda. "Actually, I'm glad you're here. There's something I want to discuss with you."

"Me?"

"Yes, you."

Julie looked torn between running off to find Alan and staying to hear what her uncle had to say.

"Shoo," Paul said. "This is for Brenda's ears only."

When they were alone and Brenda was sitting in an office chair, Paul went over to his file cabinet. He removed a manila folder, took out a newspaper clipping, and handed it to Brenda. "I want you to read this story."

It was from the *Atlanta Journal* and was dated from the summer. There was a color photo of a smiling teenage boy with a mop of curly brown hair, surrounded by Atlanta Braves baseball paraphernalia. The headline read: DREAMS COME TRUF FOR CANCER VICTIM. Brenda began to read

"It started when I was in seventh grade," says seventeen-year-old Douglas Drake as he sits in his room decorated with Braves mementos. "Aches in my joints, bruises on my arms and legs for no reason. When I first went to the doctor, he thought my folks might be abusing me." Doug chuckles over this. "My folks are the best. They've always been there for me. Anyway the doctors ran tests and told us I had leukemia.

"I went through every treatment known to science, and maybe a few that aren't. Doug leans forward, his green eyes full of mischief. But his amusement fades. He leans back in his chair and gets a faraway look. "The doctors have done all they can for me. Now that my bone-marrow transplant has failed, they've sent me home to die."

Without a shred of self-pity, Doug smiles. "I guess we all have to die sometime," he says. " 'Course, I'd rather be seventy than seventeen, but who gets to pick these things?" He doesn't wait for an answer, but adds, "The worst part for me is having to give up all the things I like to do Like baseball. I played Little League until I had to quit. And school, too. I miss going to school."

Doug has been a homebound student off and on since he was thirteen. Although he'd hoped to return to Oakbriar High for his junior year, he wasn't well enough when school opened in September. "I attended some last year," Doug says. "Long enough to know I wish I could go back."

Because of Doug's circumstances, his family's church and some community clubs have banded together over the years to help his family in many ways. An area chapter of the Make-a-Wish Foundation offered him the wish of his choice, and Doug asked to attend the Braves training camp last spring.

Doug says, "It was really great to hang around with some of my heroes. They treated me like I was special—gave me signed baseballs, a letter jacket, all kinds of stuff."

Brenda glanced up at Paul. "It's a sad story. Do you know him?"

"He had his transplant in this hospital a year ago. I got to know him because whenever he was hospitalized, he helped with the younger kids on the floor. Sort of a big-brother type. When they felt scared or didn't want to come to therapy, Doug often

brought them down and stayed with them."
He paused. "Do you remember him from
your school?"

Brenda shook her head. "Sorry, no. But
Oakbriar's huge. It's hard to remember
who's in my classes, much less who I pass in
the halls."

Paul nodded. "Actually, Doug's a patient
here now. He has a stubborn infection."

"Oh, gee, is he—I mean, how's he . . ."
Flustered, Brenda didn't know how to com-
plete her question.

"He's doing all right this time. But there's
nothing his doctors can do except patch him
up and send him home. They can't cure
him."

"What's that got to do with me?"

"He's seen you here with Julie. And he
remembers you from school. He thinks
you're beautiful. In fact, his exact words
were, 'Paul, she's the most beautiful girl I've
ever laid eyes on, and I'd give anything in
the world to meet her.' "

Two

Brenda felt a slow flush creep up her cheeks. "Me? He thinks I'm beautiful?"

Paul nodded. "He's talked about you to me every time he's seen you here with Julie. He wants to meet you, but he's shy about it. I'm probably out of bounds to even mention it, but he really doesn't have a lot of time left."

Brenda felt hot and cold at the same time. She thought it almost creepy that someone — Doug, whom she'd never *seen* — had been looking at her, thinking about her, adoring her, without her knowledge. She wasn't sure how to tell that to Paul. "Tell him hi for me, I guess."

"Would you consider meeting him?"

"Gee . . . I don't know."

"I've made you uncomfortable, haven't I?"

Brenda squirmed and stared down at her hands. "Maybe just a little." Still, she didn't want Paul to think she was insensitive. "Can I think about it? I mean, just for a day or so. I'm sure Julie will want to come see Alan again soon."

"Sure," Paul said with an encouraging smile. "Think it over. Talk about it with your friends. Whatever. I didn't mean to pressure you, but I thought I could do Doug one small favor. He's a great guy, Brenda."

She stood up self-consciously, told Paul goodbye, and went out into the hall. She looked both ways, but saw only a few therapists and a nurse around the entrance desk. There was no boy looking at her.

Brenda shook off a feeling of vulnerability and hurried to the sitting area to wait for Julie. Once they were driving home together, Brenda shrugged off her friend's questions about her meeting with Paul. In-

stead, she asked Julie about how thing
went with Alan. The ploy worked. In mi
utes Julie had forgotten all about Brenda
meeting with her uncle and was talking h
head off about the great and wonderf
Alan-of-the-blue-eyes-and-dimpled-smile.

On Saturday Brenda went to work at th
frozen-yogurt booth in the food court at th
mall. She had taken the weekend job in Se
tember, and Julie had surprised her by a
plying and getting hired also. This mornin
the mall buzzed with shoppers. Across fro
the booth, workmen had cordoned off a
area and were erecting and decorating a g
ant Christmas tree.

Suddenly Julie nudged Brenda. "Cu
guy alert."

Brenda looked up to see Matt Forreste
and a couple of his friends heading towar
the booth. Her heart skipped a beat. She an
Matt had attended the same middle schoo
and, although he had been a year ahead o
her, she'd had a secret crush on him. Now h
attended a military academy, but anyon
who followed high-school football knew tha
Matt was one of the top players in the stat

Brenda often cut out photos of him from the newspaper and stashed them in a drawer at home.

"What's the flavor of the day?" Matt looked straight at Brenda as he asked his question.

"Pumpkin Caramel. Want a taste? It's free." She reached for a little pink tasting spoon, hoping she wouldn't drop it from her trembling hands.

"Only if you feed it to me."

She felt her cheeks growing warm and wished she could think of something cute and flirty to say. Instead, her tongue felt glued to the roof of her mouth.

One of Matt's friends said, "Maybe she's not allowed to feed the animals."

Everybody laughed, which helped put Brenda at ease.

"I don't bite pretty girls," Matt said, his blue eyes staring into hers.

Brenda handed Matt the tasting spoon and he licked it clean. "What's your favorite flavor?"

"I guess I like the White Chocolate."

"I'll have that, then."

Brenda scooped frozen yogurt into a cone.

He took a lick. "Delicious. Thanks for the recommendation."

After his friends had bought cones, Matt turned back to Brenda. "You work here on the weekends, don't you?"

"Yes."

"I've been noticing," he said. "See you next time."

She watched him and his friends walk away and exhaled.

"Oh, wow!" Julie flopped against the wall dramatically. "Matt Forrester is interested in you. That is too much!"

"Julie, stop it," Brenda said, all smiles. "He is not."

" 'Only if you feed it to me.' 'I don't bite pretty girls.' 'See you next time,' " Julie quoted. "I think he's *way* interested. Wait until I tell everybody at school."

"Don't you dare. This is just between us." Brenda cast a longing glance into the food court, but Matt and his friends had disappeared.

On Monday Brenda rode back to the hospital with Julie. "How much longer is this

elationship going on?" Brenda asked.
You're killing my study life."

"As if!" Julie said.

"I'll be in the lounge," Brenda said when
hey were inside the building and Julie was
urrying off to find Alan. Brenda sighed and
lopped her books onto a table. Then she
emoved her jacket and settled into a chair.

"Is this seat taken?"

The male voice startled her. She looked up
nto the greenest pair of eyes she'd ever seen.
The boy had a curly mop of brown hair and
a gaunt, pale look that made his face look
ingular. She knew instantly who it was. "I
guess not," she told him.

He sat slowly, as if it were an effort to
nove his body. "My name's Doug Drake,"
ne said. 'And this isn't a chance meeting.
I've been hoping you'd show up again,
Brenda. Paul told me he'd talked to you
about me."

Her cheeks felt warm. "He showed me
your newspaper article. It was . . . good."

"I felt better then." He flashed her a grin
that made his face light up. "You must think
I'm idiotic to go on about you to Paul."

"No, I don't." She wanted the awkwar[d] ness of the situation to go away. "It—it w[as] sort of flattering."

"It's all true. I meant every word. I thin[k] you're so incredibly pretty."

Her embarrassment deepened. "Tha[t's] nice of you to say."

"Once I knew that you'd heard how I fe[lt] I thought I should introduce myself, so yo[u] wouldn't think the worst about me. I mean, [a] girl shouldn't have to hear through th[e] grapevine that someone thinks she's special[."]

Brenda felt like jumping up and runnin[g] out of the room. She didn't know how [to] respond. "So, how are you?"

"Pretty embarrassed," Doug confessed. "[I] didn't mean to put you on the spot."

"It's all right. Really."

Doug stood and rested his hands agains[t] the back of the chair. "I guess that's all [I] wanted to say. I'm sorry I didn't come righ[t] up to you at school last year and talk to yo[u.] I'm sorry I waited till now. Now, whe[n] there's no time left."

Brenda felt all the air go out of her lung[s.] "I've got time."

He backed away. "But I don't."

Three

Brenda arrived home from school on Thursday and found a note from her mom saying she had taken Howie, Brenda's eight-year-old brother, to the dentist. The phone rang just as Brenda scooped an apple out of the refrigerator.

"May I speak with Brenda Scolari?" a pleasant-sounding woman's voice asked when Brenda grabbed the receiver.

"Speaking."

"Brenda, I'm Florence Drake—Doug Drake's mother."

Brenda swallowed. "Yes."

"Doug told us about meeting you."

"Um—yes. We met at the hospital."

She heard Mrs. Drake let out a long sigh. "Please don't think me presumptuous for calling, but I—I really want to talk to you about my son."

"Has something happened to him?" Brenda felt a sudden chill.

"They released him from the hospital yesterday. He's at home and resting. But he's pretty down . . . you know, depressed."

"I'm sorry. But it's good that he's home again."

An awkward silence followed; then Mrs. Drake said, "I have a big favor to ask of you."

Brenda's heart hammered. She sensed the magnitude of the moment. "What favor?"

"Would you please consider going out with Doug? A date with you might make all the difference in the world to his frame of mind."

"You're trying to arrange a date between me and Doug?"

"I know it's a lot to ask," Mrs. Drake said hurriedly. "But it would mean so much to him. And his father and I would make certain you'd have a wonderful time—"

"I—I don't want to go out with Doug. I don't even know him. I've only met him once."

"Please. The two of you could do anything you want. We have the money to make sure you have a good time together."

Speechless, Brenda thought about disconnecting the call but realized Mrs. Drake might simply call her back. "I—I'll think about it," she managed to stammer.

"Oh, thank you, Brenda. Thank you.'

Brenda hung up, numb and still in shock. Doug's parents were trying to buy her! Were they crazy? An arranged date with a boy she hardly knew, and to whom she felt no attraction? What was she going to do?

That night, as Brenda was loading the dishwasher, she told her mother about the situation and Mrs. Drake's request.

"What did you tell her?" her mother asked.

"I told her I'd think about it."

Her mother looked pensive. "It is a strange offer, but as a mother, I can totally understand."

"You can?"

"Despite what kids believe, parents aren't out to make their kids' lives miserable. At least not all the time." She smiled. "I'm sure Mrs. Drake is grabbing at any straw to help her son be happy again. I'd do the same for you or Howie if either of you was in those circumstances."

"I guess . . ." Brenda could see what her mother was saying. On a smaller scale, wasn't that what she was doing to aid Julie with her flirtation with Alan? People did favors for friends. And for people they loved. Mrs. Drake's request was understandable. But Brenda still didn't want to do it.

"And you've met this Doug?"

"Once. We were both embarrassed."

"I can see where he's coming from," Brenda's mother said. "You *are* pretty special."

"Oh, Mom." Brenda waved off the compliment. "You're my mother."

"Well, Doug's mother thinks he's special, too." Brenda's mother studied her face. "You really aren't flattered by all this, are you?"

"I'm just not crazy about going out with some guy I don't know who's got cancer. I wouldn't even know what to say to him.

Cancer is awful. I still remember how things were for Grandpa, even though I was only seven."

Her mother nodded and looked sad. "It was very unpleasant, yes. In the end, he was in such pain."

Brenda recalled vividly the images of her grandfather's final months. Grandpa in the hospital with all kinds of tubes running out of him. Grandpa back home in a special hospital bed set up in the living room. People from the hospice helping Grandma care for his wasted body. The smells, the fear, the ugliness of his dying, all came back to Brenda in a rush. She would never forget it. "I don't think I could stand being around someone dying like that again."

"No one would want to," her mother said. "If they had a choice."

Brenda told herself that she had a choice. And she didn't choose to date a boy with cancer. Nor did she want to watch him die.

"You're going out with Doug? Why did you change your mind?" Julie had stopped wiping down the countertop of the yogurt booth after Brenda's announcement.

"I talked it over with my parents. They both thought I should do it. Then, after Doug's mom talked to mine on the phone and she made it sound so important to her, I felt ashamed about saying no. Besides, like my mom says, it's just one date. No big deal."

Julie put one hand on Brenda's shoulder and her other hand over her heart. "You've restored my faith in good-deed doing. Uncle Paul will be really glad, too."

Brenda flashed Julie a smile. "Does this mean I get a certificate, like the Tin Man in *The Wizard of Oz*?"

Julie had stopped listening. "Don't look now, but here comes the real man of your dreams."

Brenda looked up and saw Matt heading their way. Her breath caught in her throat.

"Got any White Chocolate?" he asked.

"A whole five gallons," Brenda answered.

"If I buy us a couple of cones, can you join me?"

"I can handle things by myself," Julie said, giving Brenda a shove. "We're not busy at all. Go, girl."

Minutes later Brenda found herself sitting

at a table with Matt, eating a frozen yogurt. She barely tasted it. Being this close to Matt had turned her thoughts to mush.

"I told you I'd be back," Matt said with a grin.

"It's the great yogurt, I'll bet."

"It's the great yogurt server." He leaned forward. "So tell me about yourself."

She decided against mentioning they'd gone to middle school together. "What do you want to know?"

"Like your name, if you have a guy in your life, what you want to be when you grow up."

"Brenda Scolari; no; and the president of my own company."

He laughed. "I like a girl with big dreams."

"You must have some big dreams yourself. With football and all."

"A college scholarship. I'm getting offers."

She was so engrossed in their conversation that she didn't see the crowd gathering around the yogurt booth until Matt mentioned it. She jumped to her feet. "I'd better go."

Matt rose with her. "Before you run off,

how about your phone number? I'd like to call you sometime."

She scribbled her number on a napkin and all but floated back to the booth.

"Are you sure you're all right about this?"

"Yes, Mom. It'll be fine." Brenda was in her room, putting the finishing touches on her makeup. Now that everything had been arranged, she was resigned to going out with Doug. His parents had gone to a lot of trouble to make the evening special, and she didn't want to act like a brat about dating someone she hardly knew.

"I hope Doug isn't disappointed," Brenda said, running a brush through her long, shiny blond hair. "I'm not some superstar or anything."

"Well, you look lovely. I'm sure he won't be disappointed."

However, Brenda was disappointed about something she couldn't even mention to her mother. Matt had had her phone number for a week and he'd never called. Nor had he stopped by the yogurt booth that day. She'd looked for him until quitting time, but he'd never showed. So she'd come straight home and dressed for her date, determined to put Matt out of her mind and concentrate on having a good time with Doug. Doug was a stranger, but he seemed to care more about her than Matt did. How hard was it to pick up a phone?

"He's here!" Howie's shout echoed up the stairs. "And he's in a car as long as our driveway!"

"What?" Brenda hurried to the window and peeked through the blinds. A gleaming white limousine sat by the curb. "A limo?" She groaned inwardly. What was Doug thinking? You didn't pick a girl up in a stretch limo for a casual date.

"He certainly does things in a grand style," her mother said, peering over Brenda's shoulder.

"I hope none of my friends see me."

Mrs. Scolari smoothed Brenda's hair. "Who cares what anybody thinks? Go have fun."

Brenda took a deep breath to calm the butterflies in her stomach, and headed for the stairs.

Four

At the foot of the stairs, Brenda paused. Her father and Howie stood talking to Doug, who was dressed in a white dinner jacket. She was grateful that for once she'd listened to her mother and worn a nice dress.

Doug looked up at her. "Wow. You look beautiful."

After small talk with her parents, Brenda walked with Doug to the curb, where the white stretch limousine waited. A uniformed chauffeur opened the car door for them. "I'd have been happy with a Ford," she joked.

"My dad's idea." Doug shrugged. "I agreed because I wasn't sure I'd ever get another opportunity to go out this way. And especially with you."

She realized this date probably wasn't easy for him, either. After all, regardless of his interest in her, they were strangers. His parents had coaxed them into this. "I'll suffer." She climbed inside the luxurious car.

The chauffeur shut the door. "But just so you'll know," Doug said, "*I* planned the date. Everything we do tonight is what *I* want to do with you. Where *I* want to take you. They left all that up to me."

The intensity in his voice touched her. They sat in an awkward silence, and Brenda realized it was going to be a very long night if they didn't start talking. "So—" they said in unison, then burst out laughing.

"You first," Doug said.

"In the article Paul showed me, it said you couldn't go to school, but that you wanted to."

"I'm in the homebound program."

"What's it like?"

"Lonely. But I get a lot of work done. That's how I've been able to stay on grade level in spite of all my hospital time. But I'd still rather be attending classes every day."

She wondered why he was even trying
keep up with his studies, given his prognosi
but didn't know how to ask.

"You want to know why, don't you?"

Had Doug read her mind? Brenc
flushed, grateful for the semidarkness of tl
car. "I guess I do."

"Attending classes is a sort of measure
normalcy for me. I've been in and out
hospitals, doctors' offices, and treatmer
protocols ever since I was thirteen. I have
network of friends in those places. We e-ma
to stay in touch, but there's nothing like tl
real world to make you feel like a regula
person. And sometimes feeling regular is tl
best medicine of all."

She couldn't imagine what it would be lik
to be stuck in hospitals. "My grandfathe
was sick when I was younger. I—I don
have good memories."

"Most people are put off by illness. I don
blame them. I've been fighting leukemia fc
so long that sometimes I forget that the re:
of the world isn't. I've read everything I ca
about my kind of leukemia." He gave a hu
morless laugh. "I could probably pass a mec
ical exam on it."

Doug took her to a restaurant atop one of the highest buildings in downtown Atlanta. The room was circular, with floor-to-ceiling windows, and below, city lights shimmered in all directions. Their table for two was set with pale-blue linen, ivory-colored tapers, and plates trimmed in gold. A single pink rose in a crystal bud vase stood between the candles. "This is beautiful," she said.

"I read in a magazine once about all the rich and famous people who've eaten here. I've always wanted to come, but not by myself. I wanted to bring someone special. I just never dreamed it would be you."

Flustered, Brenda buried her nose in her menu. Fleetingly she wondered what it would be like to be here with Matt, then scolded herself for thinking about him instead of Doug.

They ate wonderful food while a strolling violinist played. Brenda felt as if she had entered a fairy tale. How far this was from her life in high school! She was glad she'd agreed to the date. Not just because of the restaurant and limo, but because Doug was likable, outgoing, fun to be with. She knew already that she could never like him in the same way he liked her. But right now, sitting among the stars, it didn't matter.

Once the meal was over and they were riding the express elevator down, Doug asked, "Ready for part two?"

"Only if it doesn't involve food. I'm stuffed."

"Are you having fun?"

"You bet."

"Good," Doug said. "Because so am I." His eyes fairly glowed. "You've made me happy, Brenda. Happier than I've been in months."

She felt as if he'd squeezed her heart. Yes, she was having fun. But for her, this was just a date with a nice guy. And she didn't know how to tell him that was all it ever could be.

"Now where?" Brenda asked when they were back in the car.

"The planetarium," Doug said. "I thought it would be fun to look at the stars with you."

When they arrived, a man met them at curbside and led them into an empty theater. "Where's everybody else?" Brenda asked as she settled into a plush seat.

"There is nobody else. This is a private showing just for us."

"How did you arrange that?"

"I have my ways," he said with a wink.

"I've never been here before," she said, twisting in her seat, looking in every direction. "Are you interested in astronomy?"

"I used to think I'd become an astronomer," he said, a longing in his voice. "My dad bought me a telescope when I was twelve, and together we'd study the universe. I still do. In the summer, I set it up in my backyard. In the winter, at my bedroom window. If you ever want to come stargazing, just let me know."

"I'll keep it in mind," she said evasively.

"This date doesn't have to end tonight, you know."

"Doug, I—"

"It's all right," he said quickly. "I know you have a life that doesn't include me. But thank you for tonight. Even if it was a mercy date."

"A mercy date?"

"You know, a girl agrees to go out with a guy just because she feels sorry for him. Sort

of like a cousin fixing you up with a blir
date, and your having to go just to plea
your cousin."

She laughed but felt self-conscious b
cause what he'd said was true. "Well, I o
feel sorry about your being sick. But I'
having a great time, too."

"If I were able to go to school, I woul
have asked you out on my own. I know m
parents pushed you into this, but I can't sa
I'm sorry they did." His openness an
sincerity gave Brenda warm, fuzzy feeling
but that was all. She liked Doug, but ce
tainly not in the same way he liked her.

Just as the lights went down, Doug pr
his hand on top of hers. "Maybe sometim
if you want, you could come visit me. I g
lonely." He averted his gaze. "That sounc
like a pity party, doesn't it? And I don't war
you to feel sorry for me. I just enjoy you
company."

She knew he had every reason to fe
sorry for himself. It didn't seem fair that h
should be facing death before he'd ever ha
a chance to live. She couldn't tell him no
"Um—I could do that."

In the semidarkness of the theater, Brend

could almost feel his smile. "Can I call you? You won't mind?"

"Sure, you can call."

"I will," he said. "I'll call you soon."

Brenda knew positively that this was one guy who would keep his word.

Five

"Tell me *all* about it. Spare no details."
Julie sat cross-legged on Brenda's
bed Sunday afternoon while Brenda dressed
for work. Julie had driven over to pick her
up and was pressing for information about
the date.

"Doug thought of everything and made
the evening special."

"You had fun?"

"Don't sound so shocked. Of course I had
fun." Brenda described the limo, the restaurant, and the planetarium in great detail.
"Who'd have thought sitting through a show

about the universe would be fun? Not me."
Brenda answered her own question. "But it
was."

"Are you going to see him again?"

"Yes. Just as a friend. He spends a lot of
time by himself. What could it hurt to go
visit him some afternoon?"

Julie eyed her skeptically. "Are you sure
all he wants is to be your friend? Don't get
carried away just because you feel sorry for
him."

"He's not some charity case. I like him.
Really."

Julie shrugged. "Suit yourself. But don't
forget about Matt."

"I think Matt's forgotten about me,"
Brenda said with a sigh. "He's never
called."

"Maybe he'll come by the booth today."

"Maybe," Brenda said halfheartedly. Why
couldn't Matt like her the way Doug did?
She wanted to be with Matt. He was hand-
some, popular, and healthy. Health was
something she would not have even thought
about had she not known Doug. But now it
seemed like a very important ingredient.

*   *   *

"You look good enough to eat." Matt rested his elbows against the countertop and leaned into the booth to talk to Brenda. There were no other customers, Julie had taken a break, and Brenda was alone in the booth.

"Well, I'm not on the menu." Even though the sight of Matt still made her pulse race, she was irritated about his not calling.

"Ouch. I'm getting frostbite."

"Atlanta's a big place, you know." Brenda's voice was cool as she attempted to be aloof.

"Is there someone else in your life?"

"Would you care if there was?"

Matt straightened. "There is, isn't there? Who is he? Tell me about him."

Still miffed, Brenda said, "His name's Doug. We're friends."

"Just friends?"

She was afraid she might have gone too far. She didn't want to scare Matt off. "Yes. Friends."

"Good thing I'm not the jealous type," Matt said with a disarming grin.

She felt a twinge of disappointment. A little bit of jealousy meant a guy cared. Obviously Matt didn't. "Then I won't break off any of my other relationships."

"Fair enough. But do you still have room in your life for me?"

"I'm not sure you've got time for me." She didn't have the courage to add, *You never call.*

"I've been busy," he said with a shrug. "I do the best I can."

Had she insulted him? She hadn't meant to. "It's nice of you to come by to see me," she added quickly. "Can I get you a cone? My treat." She wanted to keep Matt talking. Maybe he'd ask her to do something after work.

"Not today." He stepped back from the booth.

Brenda searched for a cute remark, anything to make him stay. Her mind went blank.

A woman approached the booth, studied the menu tacked to the wall, then gave Brenda an impatient look. "I have to get busy," Brenda told Matt. Still, she hung back expectantly, giving him every opportunity to ask her out. But he didn't. He only smiled and waved goodbye.

Later, Brenda fumed and griped to Julie, "Why doesn't he ask me out? He comes here, he flirts and teases, but he never follows through. It's making me crazy."

"Why don't you ask him out?" Julie suggested. "How about to the Christmas dance?"

"Me ask Matt Forrester to the Winter Fantasy?" Brenda wondered if Julie had taken leave of her senses. Other than the prom, the Winter Fantasy was their high school's biggest formal dance. Posters about it were all over the walls at school and a big article had appeared in the student paper. The year before, she'd gone with Tyler, but now that he was out of the picture, she had no one to take her. The dance was only three weeks away.

"Why not? It's not as if a girl asking a guy is never done."

"But I've never asked a guy out before." Brenda chewed on her lower lip. "What if he says no? That would be so humiliating."

"You sat with him in the food court."

"That's hardly a date, Julie." Brenda shook her head. "It would be easier if he'd ask me out first. Then I wouldn't feel so awkward."

"You might as well know something," Julie said after a pause. "When I was coming back from my break, I saw him walking with another girl."

Brenda's heart fell. "Who?"

"Never saw her before. But she was pretty. And they were really into their conversation."

"Thanks for the day brightener'

"Don't grouse at me. I was just giving you a report."

Ashamed she'd growled at her friend, Brenda said, "I know. It's not your fault. It just makes me wonder what's going on. I can't figure out why he even bothers with me."

"Who can figure guys out?' Julie said with a shrug. "Can't live with them. Can't live without them."

Brenda agreed with a nonchalant toss of her head, but when the next customer asked for a cone, she attacked the vat of frozen yogurt with a vengeance that bent the scoop.

Six

By the end of the week, Matt had still
not called Brenda, but Doug had
called her twice. On Friday afternoon, she
drove to Doug's home, determined to put
Matt out of her mind and concentrate on
being a friend to Doug.

His house was on a quiet, tree-lined street.
November winds had blown bare the tree
branches and swirled colorful leaves into
piles along barren flowerbeds and a brick
walkway. A cluster of Indian corn hung on
the front door, and a windsock fluttered
from a porch post. The door was answered

by a short, slim woman with black hair and vibrant green eyes.

"I'm Florence," she said with a smile that resembled her son's. "Come in. I'm so glad to finally meet you, Brenda."

"It's nice to meet you too, Mrs. Drake."

"Doug's downstairs in the family room. He's a little under the weather today, but he has been looking forward to your coming from the minute you called."

"Well, if he's sick—"

"Oh, no, no," Mrs. Drake said hastily. "It's all right. It's just the way things are for him. Good days and bad days."

Hesitantly Brenda followed her to the family room. Doug was on the sofa watching TV, but he quickly turned it off and struggled to his feet. "Brenda! Boy, I'm glad you're here. This day seemed endless until now."

He looked pale, but his eyes were bright with anticipation. "Let's sit," she said, patting the sofa, half-fearing he might fall down if he didn't.

"I'll leave the two of you alone," Doug's mother said. "I've got brownies in the oven.

They should be ready soon if you'd like some."

"Fine, Mom."

"And if you want anything—"

"Bye, Mom." Doug shooed her away. Alone with Brenda, he said, "Don't mind my mom. She gets a little carried away sometimes. But you know that firsthand."

"She said you're not feeling good. Maybe I should come another day."

"No, stay. I feel better now that you're here."

She looked around the spacious room. Along one wall, there was a massive entertainment center filled with all kinds of electronic equipment. In one corner was a wood-burning stove; in another, a kitchenette. A sliding glass door led out to a patio. "Nice place," she said. "I've seen department stores with less stuff."

He smiled sheepishly. "My parents have tried to make the house as much fun as they can for me, since I sometimes have to spend whole months cooped up here."

"You have your own jukebox?" Near the kitchenette stood a large Wurlitzer, bands of colored lights glowing from its front.

"One of my father's brainstorms. But I like it—no commercials like on the radio."

"And the pinball machine, that's neat too. I couldn't live around so much temptation myself. All I'd do is play." She went over to his computer setup. "This is nicer than the ones we have at school."

"It lets me tap into the computers at the school library. My teachers post my assignments on e-mail. I can keep up on what's happening at school. Did you know that our student newspaper is online?"

"I sure didn't." She returned to the sofa. "With all these gadgets, I'll bet you have friends over all the time."

"What friends? When I was on chemo, I was real susceptible to infection, so I had to be careful about germs. After the bone-marrow transplant, security was even tighter. A cold could have slapped me back in the hospital. Or worse. So I couldn't be around too many people. Friends get busy. They forget about you. Like I told you, most of my friends are ones I've met in the hospital. And some of them have died. I miss them."

She felt sorry for him and thought it a

shame that his school friends had deserted him.

"How did we start talking about such depressing stuff anyway? You came over visit and I'm glad you did. Would you like play a video game?"

Relieved that he'd changed the subject Brenda gave him a playful poke with h finger. "Oh, sure. You practice all the tim I'll get trounced. Forget it."

"Then what do you want to do?"

They spent the afternoon listening to CD on the jukebox and talking. By that evening Doug was feeling better, and his mother in vited Brenda to stay for dinner. The mea was served in the dining room, on beautifu china plates, and Brenda wondered if tha was for her benefit. At her house, with he family's busy schedule, they usually gath ered around the kitchen table and ate fro take-out cartons.

Doug was an only child. In the course o the meal, Brenda learned that his father wa an engineer with a major airline headqua tered in Atlanta. Mrs. Drake had given u her secretarial job when Doug had gone i for his bone-marrow transplant. Brenda ce

tainly understood why they would do anything for their son—including arranging a
date with her. Her own mother had been
correct when she'd said that parents try hard
to make their kids happy.

When the meal was over, Brenda offered
to help clean up. Doug's mother wouldn't
hear of it, so she thanked his parents and
told Doug, "I really should get on home. I
have to work tomorrow."

"Before you go," he said, "come back
downstairs with me. I want to show you
something." In the family room, he held up
her jacket. "Put this on and come outside for
a minute."

Curious, Brenda slipped into her jacket
and went out onto the brick patio with him.
A hedge bordered the bricks, and a cobble-
stone path wound across the grass. A tall
wooden fence enclosed the backyard. Twi-
light blurred the edges of the yard, and overhead the sky was turning from pink to
plum-purple and to black. "Look up," Doug
said. "There's the first star." He pointed at
one lone twinkling star ascending on the horizon. "Quick—make a wish."

Brenda shut her eyes and silently wished

that Doug would get over his crush on her in a hurry. Although she thought he was really nice, her mind was filled with dreams about another. She turned to him. "Hey, I thought you were a scientist. I didn't think you believed a star had the power to grant a wish."

"Don't make fun of the power of magic. I wished for you, and here you are."

She felt a warm, tingling sensation. Doug could say the sweetest things. "Well, you should have wished for something far more exciting."

"All right," he said slowly. "I wish you'd let me take you to the Winter Fantasy."

Brenda caught her breath. She hadn't expected this.

"You've already been asked, haven't you?"

He looked so crestfallen that she blurted out, "No. I mean, not yet."

"Then go with me, Brenda. It would mean a lot to me. I know I'm not your ideal date, but I really want to take you."

She recalled Julie's advice about asking Matt. If she told Doug yes, that option was closed. But Matt never treated her the way Doug did. Doug's feelings about her were tamped clearly on his face. How could she tell him no? "I'd like to go with you, Doug. Maybe we can double with one of my friends."

His face lit up. "You mean it? You'll go with me?"

"Sure I will." Even as she said the words, she regretted them.

"Who says it doesn't pay to wish on a star?"

Seeing him looking so happy made a lump form in her throat. Her answer had meant so much to him. But she knew she didn't feel anything for him except friendship. And no matter how hard either of them wished, she knew she never would.

Seven

"**Y**ou told him you'd go to the danc with him? Brenda, what were yo thinking?"

Julie's incredulous expression mad Brenda mad. "I could use a little suppo here, Julie." They were sitting in the foo court after work, nibbling on fresh h pretzels.

"Gee—I thought you'd get up your nerv and ask Matt."

"I'm too chicken," Brenda said miserably "No . . . I'm going with Doug." Brend gave Julie a sidelong glance. "Doug told m he was renting a limo for us—just like th one we had on our first date. I asked if he minded doubling with one of my friends. He said to do whatever I wanted."

Julie gave her a blank stare; then her whole face brightened. "You mean *me*? You want me and Kevin to double-date with you two?" Julie had agreed to go with Kevin because Alan didn't want to go to a lowly high-school dance. Fortunately, Julie's crush on Alan had faded with his refusal.

"Would that be so terrible?"

"Are you kidding? It would be a lifesaver! I wasn't looking forward to an evening alone with Kevin."

Bemused, Brenda jabbed Julie in the ribs. "You're so silly, girl. Why go out with a guy you don't really care about?"

Julie rocked back in her seat. "You're asking *me* that question?"

Brenda felt her face turning red. "I like Doug," she said defensively. "I really do like him."

"Who are you trying to convince? Me or yourself?"

Brenda ignored Julie's question and told her she'd call her later. Then she picked up her tray and headed toward the trash con-

tainer. *That's the trouble with best friends,*
Brenda thought. *They know you too well.*

"What a nice color on you," Brenda's
mother said as Brenda stood in front of the
dressing room mirror in the department
store.

"Mother, it's pink. I hate pink. And the
style is babyish." Brenda glanced at Julie,
who had come along to help find the perfect
Winter Fantasy dress. It was Friday night,
and the dance was eight days away. And
with Christmas in just two weeks, the store
was jammed with shoppers.

"I agree," Julie said, making a face. "It's
too fussy."

"Don't both of you gang up on me,"
Brenda's mother said. "You know your father doesn't want to see something too so-
phisticated on his little girl."

Brenda rolled her eyes. "Well, I don't
want to go looking like a Barbie doll." Although she wasn't enthusiastic about going,
she couldn't let Doug down. If only she were
going with Matt, she'd feel completely different. But Matt had stopped by the booth only
once since Thanksgiving, and although he'd

flirted with her again, he had yet to give her a call.

"You've bought your dress already, Julie?" Brenda's mother asked.

"Mom's making it for me. I thought I'd look for shoes, but I can't wear heels." Julie sighed dramatically. "Kevin is eye level with me now. Heels would put me looking over the top of his head."

"How about this dress?" Brenda held up a midnight-blue velvet sheath.

"I don't know. . . ."

"At least let me try it on." Brenda quickly stepped out of the pink dress and into the other. The moment she saw herself in the mirror, she fell in love with the dress. The neck was high and trimmed with a choker-style collar of white seed pearls. Her shoulders were bared, and the dress fell in one long, body-hugging, fluidlike drape of soft velvet. A slit in the back allowed her to walk freely.

"Wow," Julie said. "Some dress!"

"It's lovely, Brenda, but your father—"

"Will like it, too." Brenda finished her mother's sentence. "Oh, Mom, I love it. Help me out. We can make Dad like it if we work together. ' Brenda turned, studying her reflection.

Her mother eyed the price tag. "It's awfully pricey."

'I'll pay for half," Brenda said. Julie blanched. Brenda had just volunteered almost half of her savings, but she couldn't help herself. She *had* to have the dress.

'It's December. You'll freeze." Her mother tried again to change her mind.

"I'll wear my coat. Please, Mom. I really want this dress. It's perfect." She saw by the look in her mother's eyes that she thought so, too.

"We'll take it home for your father's approval, but if he says no—"

Brenda clapped her hands and gave her mother a quick hug. "Thanks, Mom!"

They left the store with their purchases. And during the ride home, Brenda kept envisioning the look on Matt Forrester's face if only he could see her in the dress.

"It's beautiful, isn't it?"

"Oh, yes, Doug. Just beautiful." Brenda was looking through Doug's telescope at the full moon, a shimmery white circle of gleaming light. She saw mountains and craters on its surface. He had pointed out the Sea of Tranquility to her, so named by the ancient astronomers. "I've never seen the moon this way before. It looks close enough to touch."

He had called her at work that Saturday afternoon and asked her stop off on her way home. When she'd arrived, he had taken her onto the patio, where he'd set up his telescope. The night was cold and she was bundled in her ski jacket, but the sky was crystal clear, black as ink except for the stars and the pale fire of the moon.

"I was hoping you'd like it. That you wouldn't think it was a dumb idea to come over just to look through my scope." He stifled a cough.

She straightened and turned toward him. "I'm glad you asked me. Really."

"I'd have asked you sooner, but I don't want to monopolize your time. Let me refocus on a star," he added hastily.

She waited while he realigned the telescope, all the while thinking that looking at the stars was a romantic thing to do. But she felt no romantic stirring for Doug, as she did for Matt. He had not come by to see her at work today, either. She figured that whatever interest he had once held for her must be over. No visits, no phone calls. It didn't take a rocket scientist to figure things out.

"There," Doug said, stepping aside. "Look at this."

Brenda closed one eye and looked through the eyepiece. The star was merely a small dot of white light that appeared to quiver around its edges. She was disappointed, thinking it might have looked as exciting as the moon.

"It's farther away," Doug explained. "Thousands of light-years away. The light we're seeing probably left that star when the earth was in its Ice Age. But I think it has a beauty all its own, don't you?"

She thought about it and decided he was right. The faraway star resembled a seed pearl. Turning to him, she said, "Guess what? I bought my dress for the dance last night. It took all of my and my mother's powers of persuasion to talk my father into letting me *keep* it, but we did."

"I know you'll look beautiful. You could wear a rag and still be beautiful."

"You should have told me that sooner. I could have saved a bundle."

He laughed, then went into a coughing spasm.

Concerned, she asked, "You okay?"

"I think I'm getting a cold."

"Maybe we should go back inside where it's warmer."

"But I wanted to show you more stars."

"Seen one million-year-old star, seen them all." She took his hand. "Let's go in."

"I'm sorry," he said, turning his head to cough.

"No problem." Back in the warm room, Brenda noticed two bright spots of color on Doug's cheeks. "Do you have a fever?"

"I don't think so."

"I'd better go."

He looked despondent. "This isn't the way I wanted the evening to go." He sagged onto the sofa.

"Please, forget about it. You can't help it if you're coming down with a cold."

She started for the stairs, and Doug caught her hand. "I'll be well by Saturday night. Nothing's going to keep us from going to that dance."

That thought hadn't even occurred to her. "Call me tomorrow and let me know how you're feeling, okay?"

He nodded, then coughed again.

Brenda hurried upstairs, told Doug's mother she'd better check on him, then left for home. Her ski jacket was still bundled around her, and in minutes the heater had warmed the inside of the car, but she couldn't shake the cold feeling deep inside her bones. She was cold. Cold as the light from a million-year-old star.

Eight

Matt showed up at the yogurt booth about six o'clock on Sunday, just as Brenda was closing down. Julie had left earlier because her sister was performing in a Sunday-school pageant.

"Hey," Matt said, sauntering up. "Do you remember me?"

"Oh, yes. The guy who lost my phone number." Brenda forced herself to sound cool, even though her pulse had started racing at the sight of him.

"Ouch. I'm wounded." He put his hand over his chest and staggered backward dramatically. "Time sort of got away from me," he added with an apologetic grin. "Am I forgiven for losing touch with you?"

His disarming smile did the trick. She couldn't act indifferent toward him. "I forgive you."

"Let me make it up to you. Let's go out for pizza."

Brenda made up her mind instantly. "I have to call home and let Mom know I'll be late."

At the pizza parlor, they were shown to a booth and handed menus. Matt ordered a pizza and two colas.

"How have you been?" Brenda said once their sodas arrived.

"I've been really bogged down with football and classes. I hardly have any time for other things. I live on campus in one of the dorms, and life gets crazy in the place—water-balloon fights, shaving-cream wars—anything to break the monotony."

Surprised by his revelation, Brenda asked, "You don't live at home?"

"Not these days. My dad's company moved him to Los Angeles last year. If I'd gone, I'd have lost my football edge. Starting over out there would have set me back and cut into my chances for a scholarship to college. So I decided to board at the academy and play out my senior year. We had a winning season, and several college coaches have approached me, so it's been worth it. Anyway, when you live on campus, there's not a lot of privacy. The phones are in the halls, so the whole floor can listen in."

His explanation made Brenda feel better about his not calling. "Is it hard living away from your family?"

"It has some drawbacks. I miss them. Plus, they never get to my games, but I'm flying out over Christmas break."

Brenda felt a twinge of disappointment. He'd be gone the entire time they were both out of school. She forced a smile. "That's good. I've never been to California. What's it like?"

"Hopping. There's something to do every minute. By comparison, Atlanta's a drag. If my family had moved when I was starting out as a sophomore, I would have moved, too. But man, it all happened right in the middle of my junior year."

"It must have been a tough decision."

"It was. But it's made, and now they'[re] there and I'm here. But then, so are you."

It took a moment for his words to sink i[n] Feeling her heartbeat accelerate, she aske[d] "Is that a good thing?"

"It is from where I'm sitting." Matt fi[d]dled with the paper from his drinking stra[w] "Which brings me to something else I wa[nt] to say. Something I want to ask you, really He took a sip of his soda and leaned acro[ss] the table. "The academy is having a Chris[t]mas military ball on Saturday night and I[']d like you to go with me. What do you say Do you want to be my date?"

Brenda's mouth went completely dry. Sh[e] pictured him in his uniform and her in th[e] blue velvet dress by his side. Time seemed t[o] stand still. "I—I would love to go with you.

He slapped the tabletop. "All right. I'll ca[ll] you with the details." Then he smile[d] broadly. "And this time, I will call. That's [a] Forrester promise, good as gold."

She flashed him a smile, feeling warm an[d] fuzzy inside. She asked, "Matt, do you eve[r] look at the stars?"

"Sure. The NFL stars. Why do you ask?[""]

She didn't know, and suddenly felt silly. "Just curious."

Brenda barely tasted her pizza, and could hardly keep her mind focused on the drive home. The minute she arrived, she bounded up the stairs to her room and called Julie. As soon as she heard her friend's voice, she blurted out, "Guess what! Matt asked me to be his date for the ball at his school!"

Julie squealed. "Too much! When is it?"

"Saturday night. Oh, Julie, this is fantastic! I'm walking on air."

"Saturday?" Julie's voice sounded puzzled. "How are you going to do that?"

"What do you mean?"

"Earth to Brenda—hello. Isn't Saturday the Winter Fantasy? Just how do you plan on going to both?"

"What am I going to do?" Brenda wailed. Julie lay on her stomach across Brenda's bed, her chin propped in her hands. "It's a bummer, all right. Two dates on the same night. One with Mr. Guy-of-your-dreams. One with Mr. Nice-guy-but-so-what."

Brenda stopped pacing the floor of her bedroom. "I know what the problem is. I just don't know what I'm going to do about it."

"I could tell Doug you were in a car accident and you're on life support."

"This isn't some kind of joke," Brenda snapped. "This is serious."

"Well, it's a good bet that if you back out on Matt, you'll never see or hear from him again."

Brenda sagged onto the bed. "I'm sure you're right. How could I have done this? Honestly, Julie, when Matt looked across the table and asked me, everything else went out of my head. All I could see were those blue eyes and that hunky face. I never once thought about the ball being the same night as our school dance. I feel awful about this."

"I've given you my advice." Julie slid off the bed. "Find a way to get out of the date with Doug."

Julie left, and Brenda went to bed. She lay awake for a long time, reviewing her dilemma, but in the morning she felt just as torn about it as before. She thought about it all day at school, too. Everywhere she looked, she saw posters for the dance. It was all the girls talked about in the bathrooms,

he halls, the cafeteria, and the gym. Brenda
vas so sick of hearing about the dance and
eeling so much pressure over her problem
hat she slunk into the kitchen that afternoon
nd buried her face in her hands.

"Goodness, what's wrong?" Her mother
vas peeling potatoes at the sink.

"Mom, I've got a huge problem."

Her mother hastily wiped her hands on a
lish towel and hurried over to the table
"Tell me."

Brenda poured out her story, careful to
explain how special Matt was and what a
najor deal it was to be asked to the military
)all. Finally she leaned back in her chair and
ooked into her mother's eyes. "So that's the
story. What should I do?"

Her mother didn't say anything for such a
long time that Brenda wondered if she'd lost
her voice. Then she finally spoke: "You're
right—you have a problem.'

"Well, thanks a lot! I know that much.'

"Brenda, I can't tell you what to do. This
is something you have to figure out for yourself."

Brenda gaped at her mother, thinking of
all the times she'd had so much to say. Too

much, in fact. But now, when Brenda reall
needed some good advice, her mothe
wouldn't come through. "Nothing?" Brend
asked. "No ideas at all?"

"Sorry, honey. You have to make this de
cision on your own."

"But what would *you* do?" Brenda fe
desperate.

"What I would do isn't relevant. You mus
do what's right for you."

"I expected you to help me," Brend
wailed.

"No, you want me to solve your probler
for you. You got yourself in this mess. You'
have to get yourself out."

Brenda pushed away from the table an
grabbed her book bag from the floor
"Thanks a lot, Mom!" Her voice drippe
with sarcasm. Fuming, she hurried from th
kitchen.

Nine

"Brenda . . . Doug's sick." Mrs. Drake's voice sounded tight and worried over the phone Monday night. "It's pneumonia."

"That's terrible!" Brenda had expected Matt to call, but this news broke her heart and made a sick feeling settle in her stomach. "Can I talk to him?"

"He's sleeping, but I was wondering if you could come by tomorrow after school. We should talk."

"I'll be there." Brenda hung up the phone, a dark feeling of foreboding hanging over her. Across the room, her beautiful velvet dress hung from a hook on her closet door. She knew intuitively that Doug was not going to see her wear it.

Brenda didn't tell anyone at school about Mrs. Drake's phone call, preferring to keep the news to herself until after she'd seen Doug. As soon as she got home, she grabbed her mother's car keys and drove to Doug's. A holiday wreath on the Drakes' front door scented the air with pine, but Brenda couldn't remember ever feeling less in the spirit of Christmas.

Mrs. Drake opened the door before Brenda had even rung the bell. "Come in," she said. Her face looked drawn, and Brenda's heart clutched. "I want to talk to you before you see Doug."

"He must be really sick." Brenda's voice was barely a whisper.

"He is." Mrs. Drake took Brenda into the living room and sat with her on the couch.

A Christmas tree stood in the bay window, partially decorated. It looked half-dressed and forgotten, and for reasons Brenda couldn't quite understand, the sight of it saddened her.

"Doug's begged us not to hospitalize him. The hospital is a stressful environment, and since there's little that can be done for him except for medication and bed rest, his doctors feel he's better off here. A home nurse will stop by every day to check on him. You see, he doesn't have much in the way of natural resistance anymore. He's fought so long and so hard . . ." She didn't finish her sentence.

Dread stole over Brenda. "But he will get well, won't he?"

"Maybe." She said the word without meeting Brenda's eyes. "But what's certain is that he won't be going out Saturday night. He's going to tell you that he is, but it's impossible, believe me."

"I don't care about the dance," Brenda said. "All that matters is that he's all right."

"He really wanted to take you to that dance, Brenda. It represented a benchmark for him. And we really wanted him to be able to go. It—It'll be his last dance, I'm sure. Doug's father and I would like to reimburse you for your dress and any other expenses. I know these things can get costly—"

"Stop it." Tears blurred Brenda's vision. "The dress isn't important. It—It was something I already owned."

Mrs. Drake patted Brenda's hand. "You're a lovely girl. Thank you for making my son happy."

"I—I haven't done anything."

"Yes, you have. When Doug was younger, his dad and I could buy him things to take away some of his pain. A new video game, or software for his computer, or new sneakers. But now he wants things we can't buy for him. Acceptance, friends, a girl who'll care about him."

Brenda realized what Doug's mother was trying to tell her. She said, "Any girl would be touched to have Doug care about her. He's a nice guy and doesn't deserve to be sick. It isn't fair."

"I never thought so, either."

The two of them sat in silence. Sadness embraced Brenda and hung around her heart like unwanted baggage. How was she going to face Doug? But face him she must. "Can I see him now?"

"It'll make his day."

Brenda rose and followed Doug's mother up the stairs.

Doug was propped up in his bed on big pillows. He wore a Braves sweatsuit. His skin looked ashen and dark circles rimmed his eyes. Across the room a TV was on, and lamps glowed, bathing the room in soft light.

"Hi," he said as soon as Brenda came into the room. "I'm sorry you have to see me like this." Using a remote, he turned off the TV.

"You look good." She put on her most dazzling smile.

"I look bad and you know it."

"You're sick. You're allowed to look bad."

"Will you sit beside me? I just want to look at you." Brenda sat on the edge of his bed, and he added, "Listen, I want you to know that I'm not throwing in the towel about the dance. I'm doing just what my doctor says—staying in bed, taking medicine, eating even if I don't want to. Don't give up hope about going to that dance. I haven't."

"Doug, I don't care about the dance." Brenda knew that much was true. Not going lifted a huge weight off her shoulders.

"Well, if any other guy asks you—"

"I won't go with anybody if I can't go with you."

"What about your friends? And our double date."

"Julie and Kevin will understand, believe me."

Doug leaned back against the pillow. "I don't know why you even bother with me, Brenda. I can't give you any of the things I want to give you."

"You gave me the stars," she said, thinking fast. "No one's ever given me that before."

He reached for her hand. "When my spirit's set free, I'll ask God to let me visit the stars and learn all their secrets." His voice sounded muffled and full of longing. "Then I'll know all there is to know about the universe. Yes . . . the stars will be my consolation prize for having to die young."

Brenda could think of nothing more to say, nothing to make what he was going through go away. She felt helpless, useless. She held his hand long after his breathing became regular, his grip loosened, and he slept.

* * *

"Talk about dodging the bullet!" Julie told Brenda the next day at school. "Now you can go with Matt. 'Course that leaves me and Kevin to fend for ourselves"—Julie gave a shrug—"but anything to help out a friend."

Brenda just stared at Julie. "How can you act so insensitive? Doug's really sick. He might be dying."

Julie bowed her head and looked contrite. "I'm sorry. I—I wasn't thinking. I just figured this was a perfect way out of your problem. I didn't mean to sound cold."

On the surface, it did appear as if Brenda's problem was solved. Doug was too sick to go to the Winter Fantasy. She could go to Matt's military ball, and Doug need never know. Her procrastination had paid off. If she had called Matt and canceled, then found out about Doug, she would have sat home alone on Saturday night with a fantastic dress and no place to wear it. But all that had changed now. Except for one thing: she didn't want to go with Matt. The dream had lost its luster, the fantasy its glow.

"How can I go with Matt when I know

what taking me to our school dance meant to Doug?"

Julie offered a hapless shrug. "But what can you do for Doug now? Sit by his sickbed all evening? You can do that on Sunday. Or all next week while school's out."

"No . . . I won't do either. But I do have an idea, Julie. Doug's parents will have to help me, and so will you."

"Of course I'll help. What do you want me to do?"

"It's a fact that Doug can't go to the dance," Brenda said slowly, her mind working a mile a minute. "But with some hard work, the dance can come to him."

Ten

"Let me take your coat, Brenda. Everything's ready downstairs, and Doug doesn't suspect a thing." Standing in the foyer, Mr. Drake spoke in a conspiratorial whisper.

"Oh, my, you look beautiful!" Mrs. Drake said when she saw Brenda's blue velvet gown.

"Thanks." Brenda had run a wild race against the clock to finish her plan, then rush home and dress for the evening, but she had succeeded. It was just eight o'clock, and at school the Winter Fantasy would be starting.

"We'll never forget you for this," Mrs. Drake said. "It'll mean so much to Doug."

Doug's father said, "Why don't you go downstairs, and we'll bring Doug. He's weak, but his fever's down. Still, he's pretty depressed about having to miss the dance."

Her heart hammering with anticipation, Brenda went into the family room and the "winter fantasy" world she and Julie and Doug's parents had spent the afternoon creating. First she and Julie had called in sick to their job. Then they'd set to work. Now giant snowflakes sprinkled with glitter hung from the ceiling. Crepe-paper streamers crisscrossed the walls, and a mirrored disco ball suspended from the ceiling slowly spun around. Beams of light showered the room like stardust. A decorated Christmas tree sat in one corner, and a fire glowed in the wood-stove.

When Brenda had first come to the Drakes with her idea, they'd been hesitant. But as she had elaborated on it, they'd grown enthusiastic.

Even her own mother had been touched by Brenda's plan. "I knew you'd do the right thing," her mother had said warmly. "It's a fantastic idea, and I'm proud of you."

The only person who hadn't taken the news well had been Matt Forrester. Not that she blamed him. On Wednesday night, she'd called and canceled their date. "What?" he'd said. "Is this some kind of joke?"

She heard the noise of his dorm in the background. "I'm really sorry, Matt. I feel awful about this. I should never have said yes in the first place. I really wanted to go with you, but I have to be with Doug on Saturday night. He's so sick—"

"What about me? This dance is a really big deal. You're leaving me in the lurch."

She didn't remind him that he'd waited until almost the last minute to ask her, or that he'd never made her feel special the way Doug did. "I can't help it, Matt. I have to be with Doug."

"Well, thanks a lot." His voice was tight with anger. "And by the way, you were my second choice. My girl's parents grounded her, so I asked you. But she's the one I really wanted to take."

Brenda had had no way of knowing if he

was telling the truth or just trying to hu
her. "Then maybe you'd better go sit wit
her on Saturday night. Why should sh
spend the evening alone when she can hav
the great Matt Forrester to keep her con
pany?" She'd hung up without waiting fc
his response.

Now, standing in the family room, gazin
around at all they'd done to fix it up, Brend
knew she'd truly done the right thing. She'
have the rest of her life for the Matt Fo
resters of the world. But she only had thi
one special night with Doug.

From above, she heard the sound c
voices. "Dad, I don't want to go downstair.
I'm fine in my room."

"But your mom and I want to show yo
what we've done. We want you to tell us if i
works."

"Can't we do it tomorrow?"

As they cleared the edge of the stairwel
wall, Brenda could see Doug being helpe
down the stairs by his parents. They stoppe
just at the point where Doug could take i
the entire room.

Brenda stepped forward. The mirrorec
ball bathed her bare shoulders in sparkles o

light. "Hi," she said. "Welcome to the Winter Fantasy."

Speechless, Doug just stared. When he found his voice, he asked, "You did all this for me?"

"The only thing we canceled was the limo. Come on, let me show you around."

Doug's father settled him in the wheelchair. Doug protested, but it was obvious he couldn't navigate on his own.

"Over here is the photo center." Brenda led him to the Christmas tree, where Doug's father took several pictures of them. "And here's the refreshment table," she said as he wheeled the chair beside her to the kitchenette. "Your mother made little hors d'oeuvres and Christmas cookies." She held up a platter. "Gingerbread, my favorite." Brenda pointed in all directions. "We have music, lights, everything except the crowds—and who needs them anyway?"

"I guess we should get out of here," Mr. Drake said, putting his arm around his wife's waist and starting for the stairs. "Have fun," they called.

The silence in the room seemed deafening, and suddenly Brenda wasn't sure Doug was pleased with their efforts. Then he caught her hand and, looking up at her, said, "You're the most beautiful girl on the face of the earth."

Her heart swelled. She gave a slight curtsy. "It's nice of you to say so. But you may have noticed how I've cleverly eliminated any competition."

"Brenda, I—"

Afraid she might start bawling, Brenda interrupted. "So, what do you want to do first?"

"I just want to sit here and look at you."

"That's going to get old, Doug. I know, let's put on some music." She went to the jukebox and punched several buttons. Soft music replaced the silence.

"You know what I'd really like to do?" he asked. "I'd like to go out on the patio and look up at the stars."

"I don't know . . ."

"There are blankets in that chest over there. Grab a couple and let's go outside. Please."

"Your parents will kill me."

"We won't stay out long."

She found the blankets and an old base-all jacket. She tucked a blanket over his lap, helped him with the jacket, and put another blanket over his shoulders. She found a second jacket for herself. Then she opened the sliding glass doors and pushed his chair out onto the patio. The night was cold, but not frigid. Overhead, a thousand stars sparkled. "It's a pretty night," she said, breathing in the crisp air.

"A perfect night," he said.

Dreamy music spilled through the open door. "Would you like to dance?" Brenda asked.

"I—I can't—"

"Sure you can." Brenda lowered herself onto his lap, careful to keep the blanket secure around him and making certain that the arms of the wheelchair took most of her weight. She wrapped her arms around his shoulders and nestled her cheek against his neck. She felt his arm encircle her waist and his free hand turn the wheel of the chair.

They moved in a slow, lazy circle, clinging to one another while the music played in the starry, starry night.

Book Three

KATHY'S LIFE

One

"Chad, stop it. What if we get caught?" Ellie Matthias pushed her boyfriend away. All the lights in the house were off. The TV was on with the sound muted. The picture cast an eerie glow across the sofa in Ellie's living room.

"Come on, El . . . just one more kiss. I like being with you." Chad Wilson stroked Ellie's hair and cheek and pressed his mouth to hers.

Ellie twisted away. She couldn't let her mother walk in on her and Chad this way. Not when her eight-year-old sister, Marcy, was upstairs asleep and Ellie was supposed to be baby-sitting—alone. If Ellie's mother found out that Ellie had let Chad come over to study, she'd be grounded for weeks. "Maybe you'd better leave," she told Chad. "Mom might come home early." Ellie's mother worked evenings at a department store in the nearby mall.

"The stores close at nine," Chad countered. "It'll take her at least a half hour to get out of there and drive home. We have plenty of time." He pulled Ellie into his lap, locked his arms around her waist, and began nuzzling her neck. "Ummm, you smell good—like flowers."

"What if she sees your car?"

"I parked way down the street. The second we hear her drive up, I'll be out the back door. Now stop freaking on me."

Ellie felt ready to jump out of her skin, not only because she was sneaking behind her mother's back, but also because she was finding it harder and harder to say no to Chad. He was one of the most popular senior boys in her high school, and he was interested in her—*her*, a girl who'd never been very popular among her classmates. She felt Chad's hands move over her body.

His touch excited her, made her blood sizzle and her knees weak. But she knew she had to make him stop. Trembling, she pushed at his shoulders. "I'm not freaking. I just don't want to start anything right now. Right here. What if Marcy came downstairs?"

"You've got a million excuses, don't you, babe?" Chad sounded irritated. "I thought you loved me."

"You know I love you," Ellie said quickly. "But what's wrong with taking things slow and easy?"

"We *have* been going slow and easy for almost two months. I'm tired of you pushing me away. There are plenty of girls who wouldn't, you know."

The ultimate threat. Ellie's mouth went dry. She didn't want to lose Chad. "I'm just saying we shouldn't get too involved right this minute, that's all. I'm nervous."

"I won't hurt you, baby. I just want to make us both feel good." His hand slid up her thigh.

Ellie trembled inside and out. It would be so easy to let herself go with him. Chad loved her. He'd told her so many times when they were making out. Holding back was difficult, but still, she didn't want to go all the way with him. The idea scared her to death. She racked her brain for something to say, something that would back him off but would also keep him from dropping her. A flash of headlights shone through the curtains. "It's Mom!" Ellie cried.

"Don't panic," Chad said. He scrambled to stuff his shirttail into his jeans.

"Hurry!"

Chad planted a quick kiss on her mouth. "Next time," he said. "No interruptions." He bolted for the kitchen door at the back of the house.

Ellie followed and locked the door behind him. Then she raced back to the sofa and flung herself under an afghan just as her mother's key slipped into the lock. Ellie shut her eyes tightly and, with her heart thudding, feigned sleep.

"I'm home," her mother said, coming into the room. "Ellie, haven't I told you not to watch TV with the lights off?" She flicked on two lamps.

"Oh, hi, Mom." Ellie yawned, stretched, and sat up. "Sorry, I must have fallen asleep."

Her mother flopped into the nearby easy chair. "Why is the sound off? Is the thing broken? Because if it is—"

"No. I—I must have muted it." Ellie grabbed the remote. "No wonder I dropped off."

"Turn it off. I have a splitting headache. That's why I came home early. My supervisor said I could." Mrs. Matthias leaned back and rubbed her eyes wearily.

"Can I make you a cup of tea?"

"That would be nice. But make it herb tea. I have to be at the office early tomorrow."

Ellie darted into the kitchen, filled a cup with water, and put it in the microwave. Her hands were shaking so badly she could hardly control them. Tonight had been too close a call. As she waited for the microwave to beep, she sagged against the counter.

Her life felt out of control. Her parents' divorce in the spring, her father's moving away, her mother's struggling with two jobs just to make ends meet, Ellie's own problems with Chad—nothing was normal anymore. With Thanksgiving and Christmas coming up, Ellie had never felt less in the holiday spirit.

The microwave signaled that the water was hot, so Ellie removed the cup and fixed the tea the way her mother liked. She brought the cup into the living room and placed it on the end table beside the chair. Her mother, still wrapped in her coat, looked as if she hadn't moved a muscle. "Do you want some aspirin?" Ellie asked.

"I took something before I left the store." Her mother swallowed a sip of the tea. "Everything go all right here? Did Marcy give you any trouble?"

"Nothing I couldn't handle."

"You two didn't fight, did you?"

"Not once. I threatened to drown her hamster if she didn't mind me."

"I can't referee you girls anymore. You're going to have to get along."

"It was a joke, Mom. You used to laugh at my jokes."

"I used to not have to work day and night. But if we're going to have any kind of a Christmas this year . . ."

Ellie cringed. She knew all too well what was wrong with their lives these days.

"Did you get the laundry finished?"

"I had homework." Guiltily, Ellie realized

hat Chad's visit had chased her other re-
sponsibilities out of her head. She hadn't finished her homework, either.

"For crying out loud, Ellie, I can't do it all
by myself. I need help around this place."

The phone rang and Ellie jumped. Maybe
it was Chad. "I'll get it in my room."

"Don't run off. We need to discuss this."

"Later," Ellie called, shutting her bedroom door and grabbing the receiver.

"Ellie? This is Kathy Tolena. I called to
talk about that English project."

Ellie's spirits sank. Kathy was the last person she wanted to talk to. "It's not due for
another three weeks."

"But it counts for half our grade this nine-
week period. I want to get on it."

Just that afternoon, Mrs. Browne had as-
signed a killer project in English class. Then
she'd paired off the students and told them
to get it finished before school was out for
the holidays. Why had Mrs. Browne paired
Ellie with Kathy? Because if there was one
person in the entire school Ellie wasn't crazy
about, it was Kathy Tolena—or as Chad and
his friends called her, the Ice Princess.
Kathy had moved to Lakeland from Miami

and started at the high school, where every-body knew everybody else. At first some of the girls, including Ellie, had tried to make friends with Kathy, but Kathy hadn't been interested. She kept to herself, leaving school every day as soon as the bell rang.

"All right," Ellie said with a sigh. "How about right after school tomorrow? We could meet in the atrium. Or a vacant room."

Ellie's afternoons were free, for the most part. Marcy stayed in after-school care at her elementary school, and Mom picked her up on her way home from work. Weekdays, Ellie had a three-hour window in which to do homework and help around the house be-fore her mom and Marcy arrived home. Then the three of them had dinner and Mom left for her mall job.

"No can do," Kathy said. "I have an after-school job. I baby-sit for the couple I live with. I have to be home as soon as school's out."

Ellie's ears pricked up. "I didn't know you didn't live with your parents."

"It's a long story. Listen, wait for me in front of the school tomorrow, and as soon as the bell rings, I'll drive around and pick you up."

Kathy had her own car? Lucky girl. "I have things to do at home." Ellie didn't want Kathy to think she didn't have a life.

"I'll bring you home after we talk about our project and set up a work schedule."

"A schedule?"

"Of course. I'm really busy, and we'll have to plan around my schedule."

"What?" The nerve! Who did Kathy think she was, bossing Ellie around and telling her what to do?

"See you in class tomorrow.

Ellie heard the buzz of the dial tone. Kathy had hung up.

Two

"You sure look down in the dumps."

Maria's voice startled Ellie. She'd been so absorbed in her thoughts that she'd actually tuned out the noise in the cafeteria. "It's been a bad day."

Maria set her tray down and, settling beside Ellie, popped open her soda. "Want to talk about it?"

"Not much to say."

"I saw Chad flirting with Theresa Riggs. You two have a fight?"

Ellie knew all about Chad and Theresa. She'd seen them huddling in the hall before the first bell had rung. By lunch, the entire school knew about his defection. She swallowed the lump in her throat. It wouldn't do to burst into tears here in the cafeteria. "No fight. Maybe he's just getting bored with me."

"Too bad. I know how much you like him."

Ellie couldn't tell Maria the whole truth. Chad was bored with her always telling him no about touching her "It's okay. I'll get over it."

"Maybe he just doesn't want to buy you a Christmas present."

Maria's attempt at humor fell flat. Ellie picked up her tray. "I don't want to be late for class."

"You didn't eat any lunch."

"It tastes like cardboard." Ellie hurried out, aware that every eye in the cafeteria was on her.

After school, as she waited for Kathy, Ellie felt miserable. She couldn't think of anything she wanted to do less than discuss some stupid project. But when Kathy pulled up, Ellie's jaw dropped. Kathy was driving a brand-new sporty black convertible. "Hop in," Kathy said.

"Is this yours?"

"The Davidsons lease it for me. That's the couple I work for." Kathy eased the car into traffic and headed for the freeway.

Ellie gawked at the car's racy, lush interior. The child's car seat in the back looked out of place. "For their baby?"

"Yeah. I take him places sometimes."

"All this and they pay you, too?" Ellie was astounded. How had Kathy landed such a cushy job? Ellie thought about how hard her mother worked. It didn't seem fair. "Who watches the kid while you're in school?"

"There's a housekeeper."

"Where's his mother?"

"The Davidsons are both lawyers at the same firm, and right now they're in the middle of some really big case. They can't be around much, so it's me and the housekeeper. We take care of little Christian."

Ellie settled comfortably into the leather seat, pleased that some of Chad's friends had seen her get into the car. *Let them take that back to him,* she thought. Within a few minutes, Kathy had exited the freeway and turned into one of Lakeland's most beautiful and exclusive neighborhoods. A guard moioned her through the front gate. "You live ere?" Ellie couldn't conceal her surprise.

"Everybody has to live somewhere."

The house was a sprawling mansion, set back by a lake and accessible only through wrought-iron gates. A huge circular drive-way looped around blooming poinsettia plants and stately Sabal palm trees. Kathy parked in a four-car garage. Two bays were empty; a third held an older gray car. A side door opened and a plump, fiftyish woman emerged. "*Hola*, Kathy. Christian is up from his nap and in his playpen. Señora Pam has called to say that she and Señor Parker will not be home until very late."

"Thanks, Mrs. Garcia. This is Ellie. We're working on a project together for school."

Mrs. Garcia smiled, got into the gray car, and backed out of the garage. Ellie followed Kathy into a mud room, where they hung up their jackets. They walked through a kitchen of gleaming white ceramic tile and into a magnificent living room blanketed in plush, cream-colored carpeting. Overstuffed sofas and chairs, glass-topped tables, ceramic and brass lamps—all in shades of cream, ivory, and gold—graced the room. The whole back of the house opened onto a glass-and-screen enclosed patio that surrounded a pool of shimmering aqua water. Beyond the patio, a thick green lawn and colorful flower garden sloped down to the shoreline. There, a boat dock jutted into the gray-green depths of a lake dappled by bright Florida sunshine.

Dumbstruck by the house's grandeur, Ellie could only stand and stare.

Kathy hurried to a playpen, where a baby sat chewing on a plastic toy tiger. "Hey, Chris." Kathy leaned over and tousled the baby's blond curls.

He tossed the toy aside and stretched out his arms. "E! E!" he cried, his face breaking into a sunny smile.

Kathy scooped him up and hugged him close. "This is Ellie." Kathy waggled the baby's arm in Ellie's direction.

Ellie grinned, and Christian offered a smile that showed a couple of top and bottom teeth. "He's so cute! How old is he?"

"He'll be a year December twenty-fourth."

"A Christmas baby. How neat!"

"Let's go to my room. He can play on the floor."

Kathy's "room" was really a suite of rooms. Her bedroom was carpeted in emerald green, and in the center stood a wrought-iron bed draped with filmy white fabric. On one wall was a fireplace; on another, French doors leading out to the pool. An adjoining study held floor-to-ceiling bookshelves along with a desk, a computer, and a printer. A stereo and a large-screen TV had been built into a separate wall unit; a sofa, changing table, small crib, and toy chest completed the furniture grouping.

Ellie swallowed her amazement. Who knew that Kathy lived like royalty? "What's through there?" she asked.

"My dressing room and bathroom. Check it out if you want. I'm going to drag a few things out for Chris to play with."

Ellie passed through a giant room with built-in dressers and closets full of racks of clothes. Kathy's bathroom was flooded with light that streamed through a thick glass wall onto a sunken spa tub and a vanity sink topped with pale-pink granite.

Ellie scarcely knew what to think. No wonder Kathy had never jumped at the chance to be a part of Lakeland High's "in" crowd. Kathy really *was* too good for the lowly high-school bunch. Why would she be interested in them when she had everything money could buy? Who could compete with this?

Ellie returned to the study. A pile of toys had been heaped on the floor, and Kathy was sitting cross-legged in front of the baby, holding out a colorful plastic block. "Is this what you do after school? Play with the baby?"

"Well, I take him places. I feed him and bathe him and put him to bed at night, too."

"And for that you get to live like this?"

Kathy looked up at Ellie, her face expressionless. "Yes."

Ellie thought about her own house full of old hand-me-down furniture from her grandmother. She thought about her father, who'd moved away and was out of touch with his family. She thought about her mother, her two jobs, and how hard she struggled to pay the bills. And she thought about Chad, and how she was losing him. A lump swelled in her throat and tears filled her eyes. It wasn't fair. Why couldn't she have Kathy's life?

Three

"Is something wrong? You're crying."

Ellie turned her head to hide her sudden meltdown. "Must have something in my eye," she told Kathy. Mortified that she'd compared her life to Kathy's and felt sorry for herself, Ellie struggled to regain her composure. She plopped onto the floor. "So, how do you play with Chris? Does he talk?"

"He says a few things—Mama, Dada, 'poon—that's *spoon* and means he wants to eat. And he calls me E because he can't say Kathy yet."

Chris threw a block and said, "E, 'poon."

Kathy laughed. "Now we've done it. He wants a snack." She leaned close, touching her nose to the baby's. "You want a graham cracker?"

Chris started crawling toward the door.

Ellie said, "That's cute. I didn't know babies were so . . . well, that they understood stuff at this age."

"Sure they do. Don't you ever baby-sit?"

"Only for my sister, Marcy. All the families in our neighborhood don't need sitters. I want to get a real job, though, because I hate never having any money of my own."

"Why don't you get one?"

"Mom won't let me. She says there's plenty of work for me to do around the house. She wants me to concentrate on getting good grades." Ellie had argued with her mother several times about getting a job, but her mother had remained adamant—Ellie's "job" was attending school. "Last summer, I did yard work and housework for an elderly woman in our neighborhood," she told Kathy. "I stashed every dime because for Christmas I want to buy myself a clock radio with a CD player. It's expensive, so Mom suggested I wait until closer to Christmas, when it might go on sale."

Ellie felt self-conscious telling this to Kathy, who, from the looks of her surroundings, never had to pay for anything.

Kathy picked up the baby. "Come with me to the kitchen so I can feed Chris."

"What about your family? How come you don't live with them?" Ellie asked as she followed Kathy.

"My dad's in politics, and last summer he was given a diplomatic post in Kuwait—that's in the Middle East. It was a great opportunity for him, and he wanted to take it. I have two younger brothers. They're only in the fourth and sixth grades, so they didn't care. But I didn't want to go. So, Mom and Dad are really good friends with the Davidsons, and Pam and Parker said I could stay with them and finish high school in the States."

All the while Kathy talked, she was settling Chris in his high chair, tying a bib around his neck, and getting graham crackers from a walk-in pantry. "Don't you miss your family?" Ellie asked.

"Well, sure, but I'll go over and see them this summer. Besides, I'll be going off to college in the fall, so this is sort of like boot camp."

Some boot camp, Ellie thought. She said, "I'd love to go someplace on the other side of the world. I've been stuck in Lakeland all my life."

"You wouldn't want to be stuck in Kuwait. It's always hot."

Still, Ellie thought any place would be better. "You're lucky," she told Kathy. "My parents are divorced and we haven't heard from my father in months." Instantly Ellie reddened. Why had she told Kathy that? She hadn't meant to. "So what do you think of Lakeland High?" she asked, changing the subject.

"I think the place is very 'high school'— which is to say, very petty. I've heard girls grousing in the bathrooms and halls about the stupidest things."

"What things?"

"Like if some guy doesn't speak to a girl, or something. I saw a girl crying her heart out the other day because she had to sit home on Friday night." Kathy rolled her eyes. "Please. Give me a break. That girl doesn't know what a real problem is."

"And you do?" Kathy's attitude offended Ellie.

"I know that a dateless Friday night isn't the end of the world."

"The problem was real to her," Ellie said, in defense of the nameless girl. She knew firsthand how lonely life could be without a boyfriend.

"But it's hardly serious."

"There are a couple of private schools you could have gone to," Ellie told her coolly. "You didn't *have* to come to ours."

Kathy shrugged. "I considered them, but the private schools were too small. I just wanted to get lost in the masses."

Had Kathy just insulted her? Ellie wasn't sure. "Well, I like our school. And my friends."

By now the baby was finished eating. Squished graham-cracker gunk covered his face and hands and was smeared on the tray of the high chair. Kathy wiped him off with a damp cloth. "To each his own," she said, releasing the tray. "But I finished with high school and its petty problems over a year

ago. I'm going now just to get my diploma."
She picked up Chris and balanced him on
her hip. "Come back to my room. We need
to get started on the project. It sounds like
we both need the good grade."

Kathy swept from the room and Ellie
stared after her openmouthed.

"Why didn't she stay in Miami? Her folks
didn't have any friends down there for
Kathy to live with? Seems strange to me."
Maria asked her questions the next day at
lunch amid a small cluster of girls who had
gathered around Ellie in the cafeteria. They
were anxious to hear everything she knew
about the aloof Kathy Tolena. Ellie had
spared no details, relishing her role as in-
sider to Kathy's hitherto mysterious life.
Even Chad had deigned to come up to her in
the hall that morning and say, "I saw you
with Miss Frosty yesterday. What's going
on?"

Ellie's heart had thudded and her mouth
had gone dry from being close to Chad
again, but she had acted totally nonchalant.
She'd told him, "English project. We're
working at her house. I see now why she

hasn't got time for high school. Or for your friend Bennett, either." It was common knowledge that Bennett Mason had tried for weeks to date Kathy, but she'd shot him down with a cool "No thanks."

Chad had waited for Ellie to tell him more, but she'd smiled sweetly and walked off, feeling a perverse pleasure. Now, at lunch, she told the girls everything about the previous afternoon.

Maria sipped her soda thoughtfully. "And if these people are so rich, why use Kathy to baby-sit? Why not just let her live with them and hire a nanny for their baby?"

"It seems weird to me that Kathy would leave her school in Miami to come here. I mean, what's the difference between here and Kuwait?" Tricia said. "Both are nowhere."

All the girls laughed. Such questions hadn't occurred to Ellie, but now that her friends were asking them, it did seem strange. Why have a teenage girl baby-sit? And why was Kathy so willing to give up her life to do it? "She seems really attached to Chris," Ellie offered. "It's hard not to be. He's adorable."

"So was my brother," Ginny said. "Until he turned three and began vandalizing my room regularly."

"You going back over to Kathy's today?" Maria asked.

"Tomorrow," Ellie said.

"So keep us posted."

"Throw any good gossip our way."

"It doesn't even have to be good, girl. Just toss it."

The girls stood up together. "Got to run," Ginny said.

Watching them go, Ellie felt let down. If she was going to keep their interest, she'd have to do a lot more reporting in about Kathy. Guiltily she hunkered down in her chair. All she'd wanted was to get back into the inner circle of Chad's crowd. Now it looked as if she'd have to turn into a spy to stay there.

Four

"Is Daddy coming for Thanksgiving?" Marcy sat at the kitchen table, toying with the vegetables on her dinner plate.

"No, he isn't," her mother answered.

"But I want him to come," Marcy said.

Her mother looked irritated. "I don't know where he is. He left me no address, no way to contact him. Which I'd love to do, since he owes me two support checks."

"Are we even having Thanksgiving dinner?" Ellie asked, not too kindly. Except for school being out, she wasn't looking forward to the holiday.

"Of course we are. And don't act so

snippy." Her mother stood and began clea
ing the table. "In fact, tomorrow eveni
we're going to pick up the food."

"You aren't working?"

"Not tomorrow night. Would you plea
eat those vegetables, Marcy, and stop pla
ing?"

Marcy slumped in her chair. Her moth
grabbed up her plate. "I don't even kno
why I'm bothering to fix Thanksgiving di
ner. You two don't appreciate one thing
do." Her voice grew shrill. "Do you think i
easy for me? Working two jobs? Trying
hold our household together?" She did
wait for an answer but swept out of th
room.

Marcy started to cry, and Ellie crouche
beside her little sister. "Don't cry. Mo
didn't mean to yell."

"She's always mad."

"I think she's just tired." Ellie made th
only excuse she could think of.

"I miss Daddy."

"I know. So do I. But we don't miss the
yelling at each other all the time, do we
Marcy shook her head. "Then let's thin
about Thanksgiving." Ellie put her ar

around Marcy and chanted, "Turkey and pumpkin pie . . . oh, my!"

Marcy sniffed and mumbled, "Mashed potatoes and cranberry sauce . . . oh, my."

"Salad and rolls and beans, oh, my!"

Soon the two of them were marching around the table and chanting. Ellie kept up her bravado for her sister's sake, but deep down she knew Thanksgiving was never going to be the same again for their family. No, not ever.

"I thought we were going to the grocery store." Ellie peered through the car window at the brightly lit church.

Her mother pulled into the parking lot. "We're getting our turkey here this year."

Once the implication seeped through Ellie's brain, she cried, "You mean, we're taking charity? *Charity?*"

"Don't make it sound so terrible," her mother said. "Your father hasn't come through with any money, and there are bills that have to be paid. Or would you rather go without electricity? I do what I have to do. Try and act grateful."

Ellie slouched down in her seat while her

mother and sister went inside to pick up their frozen turkey. She kept remembering the opulent house where Kathy lived. Maybe she could take over Kathy's job in the summer, when Kathy went to visit her family. It wasn't such a bad idea. How hard could it be to take care of Chris?

Once Ellie's mother and sister returned to the car, Mrs. Matthias drove to the grocery store. In the parking lot, she handed Ellie a shopping list and said, "I've got to get a few things at Wal-Mart, so take this and meet us back at the car."

"I'll need some money."

"Use this." Her mother handed her a coupon book.

"What is it?"

"Food stamps. How do you think we've been getting by?"

Ellie didn't dare protest, but she loathed the whole idea. Only really poor people used food stamps. In the store, she quickly filled the shopping basket with the items on her mother's list and, with her heart pounding, went to the checkout line. Silently she prayed that no one from school would see her hand the cashier the food stamps.

"Napkins and paper towels aren't food items, miss, the cashier said. "You can't use your food stamps. You'll have to pay cash for them."

"I—I . . . didn't know." Ellie felt her face turning beet-red. "Um—maybe you'd better forget them."

The cashier shoved both packages aside. The woman on line behind Ellie gave her a bored stare. Ellie shifted from foot to foot, willing the bagger to work more quickly. She couldn't get out of the store fast enough.

"Hey, Ellie, what's up?" Maria's voice called from the next line over.

Mortified, Ellie grabbed her change, consisting of a few pennies and some food stamps, and stuffed them into her pocket. Had Maria seen? She didn't want it all over school that she was using food stamps. "Uh—nothing," Ellie said over her shoulder.

"Want me to take these out?" the bagger asked, motioning toward Ellie's basket.

"I've got it." With her head down and her face feeling as if it were on fire, Ellie shoved the basket toward the door "Got to run. My

mom's waiting," she said to Maria witho[ut]
looking at her.

"Don't eat too much turkey," Maria calle[d]
as Ellie hurried from the store.

Once outside, Ellie breathed in grea[t]
gulps of air, trying to regain her composur[e]
and blink back the tears stinging her eye[s.]
Humiliated and hating her life, she trudge[d]
to the car.

For Ellie, Thanksgiving Day was long an[d]
dismal. As soon as the meal was over, he[r]
mother went to her room with a headach[e]
and Marcy zoned out in front of the TV
watching cartoons. Ellie was cleaning up th[e]
mess in the kitchen and feeling depresse[d]
when the phone rang.

"Ellie?" Chad's voice said.

Her heart started thudding. He hadn[']t
called her since the night he'd come ove[r]
while her mother was at work. "It's me," sh[e]
said.

"You finished with dinner?"

"All done. How about you?"

"Not yet. My dad wanted to wait until th[e]
football game was over." In the backgroun[d]

Ellie heard whooping. "Touchdown," **Chad** said.

An awkward moment of silence passed. "Did you want something?" Ellie asked. She couldn't imagine why he was calling.

"Um—I've missed you, Ellie."

"I haven't gone anyplace."

"I know. I'm, um—sorry that I've been frosting you out. I was ticked. But I've been thinking about you."

"Is that why you dated Theresa?"

"I never liked her the way I liked you. You and me, we've had some good times together, haven't we?"

The hurt she'd felt over Chad's treatment of her began to dissolve. He was telling her all the right things, and besides, she had missed him, too. "Is this why you've called? To say you're sorry?"

"Partly. But also to ask you to go with me to Kevin Winn's party Saturday night."

She wanted to go with him very much but didn't want to sound too eager. "Who's going?"

"Everybody. The whole gang. It'll be a real blowout."

She paused dramatically. "I guess I can go."

"Good." Chad sounded pleased. "We'll have fun, Ellie. Just like old times. Let's say I pick you up about eight."

"I'll be ready."

In the background, Ellie heard someone shout Chad's name. "Got to run," Chad said. "See you Saturday night."

Ellie hung up. Elation replaced her gloom. Everybody would be at Kevin's party, and everybody would see that they were a couple again. Chad's call made up for a lot that had gone wrong in her life these past few days. She wanted Chad back. She wanted to be his girl again. She swore to herself that this time she would keep him.

Five

Chad was so late in picking Ellie up on Saturday night that for a while she worried that his invitation might have been a cruel joke. With relief, she hurried out to his car as soon as he pulled up. "Sorry," he said as she stepped into the car. "My dad and I got into it this afternoon, and he almost grounded me."

Ellie said, "No problem.

"The party should be jumping by the time we get there," Chad said. "We'll have to catch up."

Kevin lived in a house that backed onto a lake. It was an older place, with none of the grandeur of Kathy's house, but the property was isolated, making it perfect for a party. Cars and small trucks were parked helter-skelter along the road and up on the lawn. Every light in the house was on, and kids were milling around on the grass. "I guess his parents aren't home," Ellie observed.

"Good guess," Chad said, taking her hand.

Inside, the place was crammed with kids and thick with the smells of cigarette smoke and beer. Music all but vibrated the walls, and couples were dancing in an area of the family room where the furniture had been moved aside. "I'll get us something to drink," Chad shouted above the noise.

Ellie waved to Maria while she waited for Chad to return. Her friend sidled over. "I'm glad you came," she said.

"Who are you here with?" Ellie asked.

"Bennett brought me. How about you?"

"Chad."

Maria looked mildly surprised. "So you two patched things up?"

"I think so."

"Theresa won't like this."

"Where is she?"

"She went out of town with her family for Thanksgiving. I thought you knew."

Ellie shook her head, suddenly aware that perhaps Chad's invitation had come her way because Theresa wasn't available. "Oh, yeah . . . ," Ellie said. "I remember now."

Chad appeared with two plastic cups full of beer. He thrust one into Ellie's hand. Bravely she took a sip and grimaced. Chad laughed. "Come on, baby. Drink up. There's a whole keg in there."

Ellie smiled weakly and put the cup to her mouth, but she only pretended to drink.

Chad began checking out the room. Maria took Ellie's arm. "Come with me."

Maria led Ellie down a hall to where a line of girls were standing. "You need me to wait in line with you to go to the bathroom?" Ellie asked.

Maria laughed. "I can go by myself, but I noticed how you felt about the beer."

Self-consciously, Ellie shrugged. "I'll drink it later."

"I don't like beer either, so me, Tricia, and Ginny stashed some rum in the bathroom. We pour it into our Cokes, and it goes down a whole lot easier than beer."

Ellie realized that Maria was taking her to share their liquor. She mumbled, "It all tastes awful to me. I'll stick with plain cola."

"You sure? It's going to be a long night if you don't do any drinking."

"I'm just taking it slow and easy." Ellie certainly didn't want to get plastered tonight.

"Not too slow," Maria warned. "Chad's ready to rock and roll, girl. You better keep up."

Ellie managed another weak smile. When they returned to the family room, Bennett swept Maria into his arms, dipped her backward, and kissed her passionately. "Not a bad idea," Chad said, and pulled Ellie close. His breath smelled of beer, but his kiss left her knees weak. She felt his hands slide under her sweater and move on her skin.

She stepped away. "Stop it." He looked surprised. Before he could get angry, Ellie added, "Everybody's watching."

"The girl's shy," Bennett said, poking Chad in the ribs. "A guy should be respectful of that."

"Yeah," Maria said. "Can you spell *p-r-i-v-a-c-y*, Chad?"

Chad threw up his hands in mock defeat. "All right, you guys win." He turned to Ellie. "Sorry. I got carried away."

Grateful for Bennett and Maria's intervention and Chad's acceptance of it, Ellie smiled. "Let's dance."

They danced for a while, with Chad stopping to drink a beer every time a song was over. When a slow dance came on, he snuggled her against his chest and rested his cheek atop her head. "Did I tell you how much I've missed you? I did, you know. Theresa was just a sideline. Something to keep from thinking about you all the time."

"That's nice to hear." Ellie swayed in his arms, happy and content. She'd missed him so much.

"Will you come upstairs with me? I want to show you something."

At that moment, Ellie would have followed him anywhere. He led her up the stairs, down a hall, and into a room. He closed the door, shutting out most of the party noise, and flipped a switch on the wall. Black light turned the room an eerie shade of pale blue.

Chad said, "This is Kevin's room. Pretty cool, huh?"

She held out her hands and waggled her fingers. In the black light, her skin looked icy blue and otherworldly. "Neat."

Chad stepped behind her and circled her waist with his arms. "No, you're neat," he said in her ear. "I really like you, Ellie. I want you to be my girl."

Her heart hammered. Never in her wildest dreams had she expected this. She turned slowly in his embrace and slipped her arms around his neck. "I've always been your girl, Chad. From the very first time we dated."

"Oh, baby." His breath felt hot on her throat, and his mouth moved over her lips and down her neck. Her insides quivered and her breath came in little gasps.

In seconds she was lying on Kevin's bed and Chad was beside her, stroking her, kissing her, whispering of his love. Ellie felt as if she were floating on a sea of warmth. Her body ached with yearning. Chad eased her sweater higher and ran his hands across her skin. She shivered, basking in the sheer pleasure of his touch. She felt his hand slip

nside the waistband of her pants. She
sucked in her breath and tensed.

"It's okay, baby," Chad whispered. "I
won't hurt you. I just want to make you feel
good. And it will feel good, Ellie. I promise,
I'll make you feel so good."

Tension crawled up her body, steeling her
muscles, making them cramp. "We—We'd
better stop."

"I don't want to stop. I want to make love
to you. Please, Ellie. I want you so bad."

Ellie jerked his hand away and sat upright. "I—I can't. Please, stop." She was crying without wanting to.

Chad sat up. In the black light, his face
looked malevolent. "This is stupid, Ellie. You
want to be my girl, but you don't want me to
touch you. What kind of a girl are you?"

"I—I want you to touch me," Ellie stam-
mered. "It's just that I'm afraid."

"Afraid of what? I said I wouldn't hurt
you. Don't you trust me?"

"I trust you."

"Then act like it. You're tying me in knots,
baby. Don't you know how hard it is for a
guy to stop real sudden? It's painful, Ellie.
And you keep doing it to me."

"I don't mean to. I only want us to be—"

"Well, we can't be anything if you can't be here for me in every way."

Miserable, Ellie hung her head. "I just can't, Chad. Not only don't I have any protection, I can't let myself go all the way."

"Well, that really sucks." Chad got off the bed and began to weave from side to side.

For a moment Ellie thought he might fall over. "Let's talk," she said, reaching for his hand.

He yanked it away. "Forget it. The time for talking's over. I ask you to be my girl and you throw it back in my face. It's over, Ellie. I'm getting me a girl who really cares about me." Chad jerked open the door and left her alone in the room.

The sounds of the party drifted through the doorway. Shaking, scared, and humiliated, Ellie knew she couldn't go back and act as if nothing had happened. Chad was probably down there right now telling everybody what a loser she was. She wanted to hide. She wanted to run away. But Chad had brought her. Ellie started to cry. She had to get out of there and get home.

She saw a phone on Kevin's desk. She

would call someone to come get her. But who? Everyone she knew was downstairs at the party. She couldn't call her mother. Desperately, she racked her brain. Suddenly one face came to her. With trembling fingers, she dialed the number, silently praying, *Please be home.*

"Hello?"

"Kathy, it's me, Ellie." The words tumbled out in a rush. "Please help me. Please!"

Six

"Are you sure you're all right?" Kath asked, holding out a tissue.

In the safety of Kathy's bedroom, Elli sobbed openly. "Thank you for coming t get me. I—I didn't know who else to call.'

"I'm glad I was home. Tell me what hap pened."

After Kathy had agreed to pick her u from the party, Ellie had crept down th stairs and slipped out the laundry roor door. She'd waited, shivering in the darl beside the road in front of the house unt Kathy arrived. During the ride back t Kathy's, Ellie had wept quietly, and Kath had not said a word. Now, sitting cross-legged in the center of Kathy's bed, Ellie knew she owed Kathy an explanation. "I was so excited when Chad asked me to the party. I thought we were going to start over. But he—he wants me to do things with him I don't want to do."

"He wants you to have sex. Is that right?"

"Yes." Ellie was surprised by the accuracy of Kathy's assessment.

"But you don't want to."

"Not really." Kathy probably thought she was acting like a crybaby. "The girls who sleep with their boyfriends get talked about—trashed, usually. But if you act too uptight, they call you 'frigid' and 'icicle.'" She was ashamed now for not defending Kathy when she had been called those names.

"Then you're always in a losing situation," Kathy said. "Either way, you're going to be talked about."

Ellie hadn't thought of it that way. "It doesn't matter now anyway. By Monday, it'll be all over school about me and Chad."

"What—that Ellie Matthias said no to the great Chad Wilson? What's so terrible about that? I've always thought Chad was a jerk."

"You have?"

"Some of these high-school guys think they're so cool, and that any girl who doesn't fall at their feet is somehow defective. You're a smart girl, Ellie. Why would you buy into something as stupid as that kind of lie?"

Surprised by the vehemence in Kathy's voice, Ellie looked up to see Kathy's eyes blazing with anger. "I guess I never thought about it as a lie," Ellie told her.

"There's nothing wrong with virginity, Ellie. It's not a disease. You shouldn't have to apologize for wanting to save yourself for the right guy."

"But Chad made me feel—" She searched for the right word.

"Hot?" Kathy supplied. Ellie nodded. "All that proves is that you're normal. But feeling it and doing it aren't the same thing. And nobody should make you do it if you don't want to."

"Have you?" Ellie asked. "Ever 'done it,' I mean?"

Kathy gave her a bored look. "We aren't talking about me. We're talking about you

tanding up for yourself and saying no to
omething you don't want to do."

"Is that why you wouldn't date Bennett?
Because everybody expected you to?"

Kathy sighed and sat down on the bed.
'He's so 'high school'—he thinks he's so
ool. I didn't want to be bored."

Ellie admired Kathy's self-assurance and
omposure. If only she could tap into that
or herself. "I'm not sure what I should do
ow."

"I think you should sleep over tonight."

"Here?"

"No, in my car. Of course here."

"Won't Mr. and Mrs. Davidson mind?"

"Why should they? They let me do pretty
much as I please."

"I—I'll have to call my mom . . . tell her
omething about leaving the party that's be-
ievable."

"Tell her the truth—that the party got
owdy and we came to my house to avoid
rouble. It'll convince her that you're mature
nd levelheaded." Kathy smiled. "And isn't
hat just the way we want our parents to
hink about us?" She added, "I'll talk to her
f she needs proof that you're really here."

In the past, Ellie had disliked Kathy
take-charge attitude, but now she was grat
ful for it. She blew her nose, washed h
face, and made her call. She and Kathy ha
no trouble persuading her mother to let h
spend the night. To Ellie's amazement, h
mother actually praised her for "having t
good sense to get out of a bad situation."

"We'll watch a movie," Kathy said, pullin
a video from a shelf.

Ellie agreed, but she was so exhauste
that she could hardly follow the story. Sh
fell asleep on the floor with the VC
playing, all the time feeling envious of every
thing about Kathy Tolena. Why couldn't sh
have Kathy's life instead of the one sh
had?

The next morning, Ellie awoke to th
smell of breakfast wafting through th
house. She was alone in the room. Sh
dressed quickly and padded out to th
kitchen, where she met Pam and Parker Da
vidson, Christian's parents. The baby wa
sitting in his high chair, and Kathy was feed
ing him breakfast.

"I'm so glad to meet you," Pam said with

sunny smile. She wore a gorgeous silk robe and her dark hair was pulled back into a ponytail. She was making waffles on a griddle set on an island in the center of the kitchen. "I'm only sorry we haven't met you sooner, but this case we're defending goes to trial in January and we've been working night and day to be ready for it. How many waffles can you eat?"

"One to start."

Her husband folded his newspaper and set it aside. "Do you girls have something planned for the day?"

"We have a big project due at school that we're working on," Kathy said.

"Then we'll get out of your way. We're taking Chris out for a little bonding time . . . the mall, lunch, feeding the ducks down at the lake," Mr. Davidson said. "Plus, Santa's arriving downtown around three, and we'd like to take Chris for the big event."

"That is, if you don't mind," Pam added quickly.

Ellie poured syrup on her waffle and wondered why it would matter to Kathy where they took their son for the day.

"Sure," Kathy said, glancing from one to the other. "Whatever."

Maybe they feel guilty about going off and leaving Kathy alone all day, Ellie thought as she ate the waffle. "This is good," she told Mrs. Davidson.

"There are plenty more." She turned to Kathy. "If Chris is finished with his breakfast, I've got a waffle with your name on it."

Kathy wiped the baby's hands and face and sprinkled some Cheerios on his tray. He grinned and started shoving them in his mouth while Kathy sat down to eat her breakfast. Ellie giggled and told Pam, "Your son's really cute."

"Thank you," Pam said without meeting Ellie's eyes.

Ellie chewed contentedly and looked out at the pool, where sunlight resembled scattered jewels on the surface of the water. *This is what a real family is like,* she mused. The Davidsons looked happy, the baby was adorable, and Kathy had the perfect job caring for him while living in a palace without parents to gripe at her. Kathy was pretty lucky.

Mrs. Davidson released the high-chair

tray and picked up the baby. "Let's go get dressed," she said to Chris, swinging him around. "Would you like to see Santa later?"

Chris gurgled but cast a glance toward Kathy. "E," he said, turning away from his mother. "E, E."

"Isn't that cute?" Ellie asked Kathy. "He wants you."

"E, E," Chris continued to chant, clenching and unclenching his fists in Kathy's direction.

Kathy ignored him. "You go with your mother," she said quietly.

Mr. Davidson stepped in and took the squirming baby from his wife. "Come on, big guy. Let's give Kathy a rest today." He carried the fussy baby out of the kitchen.

Mrs. Davidson stood by the high chair, looking stricken. "I—I guess we've been away too much. He hardly recognizes us these days."

"It's all right, Pam," Kathy said. "Please, go on and have fun today."

Pam hurried out of the room.

In the silence that lingered, Kathy looked pensive, even somber, and Ellie wondered if she might be missing her family so far away in Kuwait. "Um—Kathy, do you want to take me home and go with them? If you do, it's all right."

Kathy shook her head, then in a no-nonsense voice said, "We've got a project to finish, remember?" She stood up and whisked the dishes into the sink. "Come on. If you want to shower, I'll find you something to wear."

"Whatever," Ellie said, baffled.

Kathy darted from the kitchen, but Ellie couldn't shake the feeling that something was going on between Kathy and the Davidsons that nobody wanted to talk about. Something mysterious. *It's none of your business,* she told herself. It did little good. Every cell in her body burned with curiosity.

Seven

On Monday at school, Ellie heard the talk. Kathy had made her feel proud of telling Chad no, but the rumor mill cranked out cruel jokes about her and brought her back into harsh reality. She was especially stung by Maria's treatment. Maria barely spoke to her, all but ignoring her when the other girls were around.

"They'll move on to somebody else before long," Kathy assured her when she discovered Ellie crying in the bathroom.

"They're spreading out-and-out lies about me," Ellie insisted. "They're saying Chad and I disappeared upstairs for hours

They're saying things happened that didn't happen. It isn't true! Why did I ever trust him?"

"Because you thought you loved him," Kathy said matter-of-factly. "It happens. Believe me, by New Year's everyone will have forgotten all about Ellie and Chad and moved on to someone else."

Ellie had counted the days until Christmas break. When it arrived, she said "Good riddance" to the school building, then got into Kathy's car. The English project was finished and turned in; they'd get their grade in January. For Ellie, the grade was secondary. What concerned her was that now she had no excuse to spend time with Kathy. And at the moment, Kathy was her only friend.

Glancing over at Kathy, she asked, "So what're you going to do over the break?"

"Take care of Chris."

"Nothing else? Any Christmas shopping?"

"I've already mailed stuff to my family in Kuwait."

"How about gifts for the Davidsons? And for Chris?"

"The one thing the Davidsons want I can't shop for," Kathy said enigmatically.

Ellie puzzled over the comment. Unable to figure out what Kathy meant, she asked, "Isn't Christian having a birthday soon? We could plan a party for him. I know he's only going to be one, but I'll bet the Davidsons have been too busy to think much about it. What do you think?"

"I guess we could," Kathy said without enthusiasm. That surprised Ellie. Kathy was usually very enthusiastic about everything that had to do with Chris. They rode in silence until Kathy asked, "Would you like to go to the mall with me on Monday?"

"Sure. But we'll have to take my sister with us because I have to watch her while Mom's at work."

"Fine with me."

Ellie settled back against the seat, somewhat pacified. So what if her friends ignored her? She would be Kathy's friend. Kathy was smart, self-confident, and nice. Who wouldn't want a friend like that? The others could go jump in the lake for all she cared.

On Monday Ellie, Marcy, Kathy, and

Chris went to the mall. Marcy took to the baby immediately, asking to push his stroller around the stores crowded with Christmas shoppers. When Kathy darted into a toy store, Ellie and Marcy stayed outside with Chris, gazing into the toy-laden display window. "That's what I want," Marcy said slowly, pointing to a colorful plastic apartment house for Barbie.

"It's expensive," Ellie said. "I doubt Mom can afford it."

Marcy stared at the toy, then sighed. "I know. I guess I'll just have to save more money."

Ellie felt sorry for her sister—for both of them, really. As far as getting presents, it wasn't going to be much of a Christmas. She was really glad she'd saved for the one thing she wanted. At least she knew she'd get it. "That's about all you can do," she said. "But if I have any money left over after I buy my radio, you can have it. It wouldn't be much," she added hastily. "Maybe a few dollars, but it'll help some."

Sounding resigned, Marcy said slowly, "Thanks . . . maybe I can get it for my birthday this summer."

Chris took that opportunity to toss his plastic bottle out of the stroller. Marcy retrieved it, cooed at the baby, and handed it back to him. He offered a big grin and Marcy laughed, her disappointment about the toy forgotten.

By then Kathy had come out of the store with her purchases. "I want to get Chris's picture taken with Santa," she told Ellie and Marcy.

"I thought the Davidsons did that already," Ellie said.

"They did, but I want *my* picture with him and Santa."

They stood in a long line, and by the time it was their turn, Chris was half asleep. Still, Kathy picked him up and nestled him in Santa's arms. She crouched down and waited while Santa's elf snapped the photo. Minutes later the elf brought Kathy a print of the picture. Kathy paid for it, then held it out, looking at it for the longest time.

"Cute," Ellie said, anxious to get on with their shopping.

"I like it, too," Marcy chimed in.

Kathy said nothing, just stood and stared at the photo in her hand. Ellie could have sworn she saw moisture in Kathy's eyes. "Um—everything okay?" Ellie asked.

Kathy nodded, tucked the picture into her purse, and said, "Sure. Everything's just fine."

Ellie traded baffled looks with Marcy. For the life of her, she couldn't figure Kathy out. Sometimes she acted assured and confident, other times sad and distant. For a girl who had everything, Kathy didn't seem any happier than Ellie, who had almost nothing. No . . . it made no sense to Ellie at all.

Five days before Christmas, the Davidsons had to fly to New York on business. Kathy asked Ellie to sleep over. Fortunately, Marcy had been asked to spend the night with a friend of hers, so Ellie was free. That night, after they'd eaten hamburgers, Kathy bathed Chris and dressed him in Santa pajamas. Fresh from his bath, smelling of baby powder and lotion, he had never looked cuter to Ellie. He was learning to walk. He'd take a few unsteady steps, then flop down and crawl rapidly toward the Christmas tree that stood in glittering splendor by a large bay window.

"No you don't, buster," Kathy said, scooping him up and redirecting him toward Ellie, who enticed him in her direction with toys.

"He sure has a one-track mind," Ellie said with a laugh. "Just like most guys."

Kathy chuckled. "Don't put that label on Chris. He's going to grow up and be different. He's going to treat girls with respect."

"If only," Ellie said. "Maybe we should both come back and check on him when he's sixteen, just to make sure."

A shadow crossed Kathy's face. She stood and picked the baby up. "Bedtime," she announced. Ellie thought her decision rather abrupt but didn't say anything. At the doorway, Kathy said, "While I'm putting Chris down, go in my room and pick out a video. We'll watch it out here on the home-theater system—it's awesome."

Ellie retreated to Kathy's suite and started riffling through the library of videotapes and laser discs on the shelves. She chose one, turned, and in her haste knocked a small box to the floor. "Oops," she said, and bent to retrieve the spilled contents. Scattered on the floor were the recent photo of Chris, Kathy, and Santa—and another of a new-

born baby bundled in a flannel blanket
Chris? Ellie wondered. It sure looked like
him.

Ellie picked up a tiny bracelet of alternat-
ing blue and white lettered beads. *B-O-
T-O-L-E-N-A*, the beads spelled. Ellie stared
her mind struggling to make sense of it
Then the light of understanding flared. She
felt as if all the air had been sucked from the
room and a weight were pressing against her
chest.

"What's the holdup?" Kathy came into the
room.

Ellie whipped around, feeling like a thief
caught in the act. "I—I accidentally knocked
this box on the floor."

Kathy's eyes grew wide, panic-stricken.

Ellie couldn't help herself. She held out
the tiny bracelet. "Is Chris *your* son, Kathy?"

Eight

With trembling fingers, Kathy took the bracelet. Tears filled her eyes as she fingered the lettered beads lovingly, like a rosary. "Yes," she whispered. "Chris is my son."

Tears welled in Ellie's eyes, too. She was overwhelmed—and unsure of what to say now that she'd stumbled upon this startling truth. "I truly didn't mean to pry. You've been a good friend to me. Now, if you need me, I promise to be as good a friend to you. Please tell me what's going on. Who are the Davidsons? Why are you pretending Chris isn't yours?"

Kathy walked to the love seat and, curling her legs under her, settled there. She clutched the tiny bracelet against her breast. "The Davidsons are Chris's adoptive parents. At least, they will be if I decide to sign the final papers."

Is this really happening? thought Ellie. "*If* you sign? You mean, you might not?"

"I should have signed the papers when Chris was born. But I didn't. You see, through my father's attorney, we'd been given the Davidsons name as a childless couple who wanted to adopt. Private adoptions happen all the time. Pam and Parker came to visit us in Miami while I was still pregnant, and I really liked them."

"What's not to like?" Ellie said. "They're really nice."

"But once Chris was born, when I held him, I just couldn't give him up. Pam and Parker were really upset . . . they wanted a baby so much. You see, Pam can't have children, so they have to adopt if they're ever going to have a family. So, rather than lose Chris altogether, they suggested that we have a kind of open adoption—where I could live with them, take care of the baby,

ven finish school. We made up the story
bout me being his sitter so that I could fit in
t school. Except it hasn't been so easy. I
lon't have anything in common with the
irls my age anymore. I mean, when you're
hanging diapers and fixing formula, it's
asy to lose interest in high-school life. And I
ure don't want to date anyone. Besides,
vhat high-school guy wants to date a girl
vith a child of her own?" Kathy stared up
t Ellie, her eyes large, luminous, and
ad.

It broke Ellie's heart. "What about your
parents? What do they want you to do?"

"It's complicated. My father really is a
liplomat. He received his appointment to
Kuwait a few months before Chris was born.
And he couldn't take his unmarried, pregnant daughter into that culture. It would
ave hurt him politically. He has a future in
he diplomatic corps. I didn't want to ruin it
or him. All along they've wanted me to give
Chris up for adoption—they never kept their
eelings a secret."

Ellie could only imagine the kind of pressure Kathy must have been under when
Chris was born—adults bombarding her

from every side with urgings to give up he
baby. "You must have been so scared whe
you found out you were pregnant."

Kathy nodded. "I was fifteen, a soph
ore, and scared out of my wits. But
knew I'd never have an abortion. I couldn
do that to my baby. It wasn't his fault h
was growing inside me. I waited until
was six months along before I told my pa
ents. By then it was too late to have an abo
tion."

Six months! That seemed like a lifetime
keep such a secret. "What about Chris's fa
ther? Why didn't the two of you get ma
ried?"

Kathy's expression hardened. "He didn
want to be saddled with a family at sixteen
You see, he was an athlete. He had big plar
for college. He had told me he loved me.
believed him. Yet when I told him I wa
pregnant . . ." Kathy paused. "Ellie, don
ever let anyone tell you that you can't ge
pregnant the first time you 'do it.' You car
I'm proof of that."

"I'm sorry." Ellie *was* sorry, but the wor
sounded inadequate. She kept imaginin
Kathy's fear and panic.

"Everyone was sorry. But it didn't change anything—I was still going to have a baby. So my dad and brothers moved to Kuwait, and Mom stayed with me until Chris was born. When I didn't sign the papers, Mom got pretty angry. But I just couldn't." Kathy turned her tortured gaze on Ellie. "That's when Pam and Parker made their offer. I took it, thinking I could move up here, finish school on schedule, and go on with my life."

"You can still do that."

"But you've found out the truth." Kathy hung her head. "I'm fuel for the gossip mill at school."

Shocked, Ellie knelt beside her friend. "I will never tell your secret. Never! You can finish out the year without being afraid that I'll say anything. I promise you, Kathy."

"Having this to talk about would certainly get you back into everybody's good graces."

Hurt by Kathy's insinuation, Ellie sat back on her heels. "I won't do it. I don't care if they never speak to me again."

Kathy managed a smile. "I'd be very grateful if you kept my secret. In six months, I'll graduate."

"Then what?"

Kathy shrugged. "A lot depends on whether or not I sign the papers."

"So are you going to?"

"I don't know. I thought it would be easier to let Chris go after a year, but it isn't. Every time Chris calls Pam Mama, it cuts me like a knife. I'm E, but she's Mama."

"So don't sign. He'll never remember the Davidsons if you move out and raise him yourself."

"Look around you, Ellie. Look at all the things they can give him."

"So they can give him a lot of stuff. It shouldn't be about giving him stuff."

"They can make him a part of a *family*," Kathy said, her voice full of passion. "I can't give him that. Pam and Parker love Chris, and they want to be his parents more than anything. Pam will quit work the second Chris is theirs. She only works now to give me lots of time with Chris, and to stay busy in case I—" She interrupted herself. "They love Chris, too. How can I take him away from them?"

There was no simple answer to Kathy's

dilemma. From what Ellie could see, there didn't seem to be an answer at all. "What are you going to do, Kathy?"

"I don't know, Ellie. I swear, I don't know what to do."

Nine

For days Ellie couldn't get Kathy off her mind. She felt so sorry for her. What a terrible choice Kathy was left to make. Ellie didn't even know the name of the boy who hadn't stood by Kathy, but she hated him for Kathy's sake. He'd deserted Kathy and his son. It didn't seem fair.

Three days before Christmas, Ellie's mother came home with good news. She'd gotten a Christmas bonus check and a promotion at her day job. Now she'd be able to quit her evening job at the mall. "What a relief!" she'd declared when she told Ellie and Marcy

Ellie was happy for her mother—for herself and her sister, too. And the change in their mother was dramatic. She smiled more and grew less tense and edgy, which gave Ellie hope that Christmas wouldn't be a repeat of Thanksgiving.

Ellie had gone to the mall for some last-minute purchases and was running out of a store when she bumped smack into Maria.

"Ellie! How goes it?"

"Fine. How about you?"

"Okay . . . a little crazy. My aunt and cousins are coming in tonight. They live in Indiana. We went up there last Christmas. Now it's their turn to come here. My cousin Shelly is all right, but the other two are sort of a pain." Maria poured on the details.

"Been to any more parties?" Ellie asked, her tone pointed. She was still upset with Maria for turning against her.

Maria turned red. "Listen, Ellie, I never believed one word of what Chad said about you after that party."

"Really? I'd never have guessed it by the way you treated me."

"I defended you. Honest. I told the others you would never have gone up to the bedroom with Chad unless he tricked you. I knew you didn't have sex with him—no matter how much he bragged that you had."

Ellie felt a sinking sensation in the pit of her stomach. The lies still hurt, but suddenly they didn't seem so important. As Kathy was fond of saying, they were "very high school." Ellie looked Maria in the eye. "He really did tell lies about me, Maria. I told Chad no, he got angry, and now he's getting even. But I'm glad I told him no. He can say whatever he wants. I know the truth. He knows the truth. I said no to the great Chad Wilson."

Maria managed a self-conscious smile. "I'll do what I can to set the record straight with the others. And, uh—Ellie . . . I'll see you at school after the holidays. Okay?"

"Okay." Ellie watched Maria hurry off, knowing that whatever happened when school started again, she would never be quite so eager to fit in with the old gang. Kathy's friendship—Kathy's life—had changed her, made her see love and commitment with different eyes. Ellie left the mall feeling better about herself than she had in weeks.

❖   ❖   ❖

"Are you sure they want *me* to come to this birthday party, honey?"

"Positive, Mom. Kathy and the Davidsons invited all three of us." Ellie sat in the front seat, Marcy in the back, as their mother drove down the quiet residential streets in the late afternoon of Christmas Eve.

"It just seems odd, that's all. I don't even know these people."

"You've met Kathy."

"Well, yes, but it's been years since I've been to a birthday party for a one-year-old."

"Chris is really cute, Mom," Marcy piped up from the backseat. "You're going to love him."

"We can't stay too long," their mother said. "I don't want to be late for church. The candlelight service is my favorite."

"Mine too," Marcy chirped.

The Christmas Eve candlelight service was Ellie's favorite also. But tonight her mind wasn't on Christmas. It was on Kathy. One year ago Kathy had been in the hospital, having a baby. A baby she loved and now had to decide whether to keep or give up for adoption.

"Turn here," Ellie told her mother.

"Holy cow," her mother said, pulling into the Davidsons' driveway. "I didn't know we were going to a palace. Did I dress well enough?"

"You look fine, Mom."

The front of the house and the shrubbery were decorated with small white lights. There was a glowing candle in every window, and two enormous wreaths trimmed with red velvet bows hung on the double front doors. "They're just regular people," Ellie said, getting out of the car. Marcy grabbed the bag of birthday gifts and followed.

After a round of introductions, Ellie and her family were taken into the formal dining room, where the party had been set up. "The kitchen seemed too casual," Pam explained. "But all of a sudden this looks too formal," she added with a laugh.

At one end Parker had positioned a video camera. Chris sat in his high chair. His blond hair had been combed in an attempt to tame his curls, and he wore a big bib that had #1 BIRTHDAY BOY emblazoned across it in bright red. He grinned winsomely, and a lump closed off Ellie's throat. How could Kathy let him go?

Kathy brought in a cake with one glowing candle. Everyone sang and Chris beamed while the video camera recorded every moment. After everyone had eaten cake and the adults had lingered over coffee, Marcy took Chris into another room to play with him and his new toys. Kathy and Ellie went ou side. They walked across the lawn and out onto the dock that jutted into the lake. A long-necked crane lifted from the edge of the water and flew above the horizon across the bright orange circle of the setting sun. The air, barely tinged with coolness, was heavy with the scent of tropical blossoms.

"How's it going?" Ellie asked.

"My parents called today from Kuwait to wish me a merry Christmas. They said that after I graduate, if I want to bring Chris and come live with them, it would be all right. They said they'd make up some story about the two of us to tell everybody."

Ellie contemplated Kathy's news. "Well, it would be a way for you to keep Chris."

"They don't really want us, Ellie. They're

just feeling guilty about the way they handled everything last year."

"But once they see Chris, they'll fall in love with him. They won't be able to help themselves."

Kathy managed a sad smile. "That's probably true, but Chris and I couldn't live with my parents forever. Eventually we'd have to come back and I'd have to get some kind of job. How will I take care of Chris all by myself?"

"Maybe Pam and Parker could adopt both of you."

Kathy patted Ellie's arm. "Nice thought, but probably not. No . . . Chris and I will have to be on our own."

"Gee, Kathy, this is really tough. I wish I could help you."

"You have helped," Kathy said with a sigh. "I'm glad to have somebody to talk to about it. Until you, I had no one but Pam. Or my parents—if I wanted to call Kuwait."

"And they all want you to give up Chris."

"I want to do what's right, Ellie. What's best for both of us."

At that moment the screen door slammed, and both girls turned to see Marcy sprinting toward them. "Mom says we have to go if we're going to get a seat in church," Marcy told Ellie.

Ellie turned to Kathy. "Do you want to come with us? It's a really nice service. Real peaceful."

Kathy shook her head. "I want to be with Chris. It's his birthday."

Marcy grabbed Ellie's hand and pointed up. "Look! The first star. Everybody make a wish."

Ellie looked up, then over at Kathy. Tears shimmered in Kathy's eyes. "I've wished on that star a hundred times," Kathy said. "I don't even know what to wish for anymore."

But Ellie did. She took Kathy's hand, looked up at the bright, glimmering star, and wished with all her heart for Kathy to find her answer. For Kathy to be at peace with whatever she chose to do.

Later, when they were driving to church, Ellie's mother said, "You know, I really had a good time tonight. I'm glad I went."

"Me too!" Marcy cried.

"And when I was talking to the David-sons, they said they might help me get the back child support your father owes.

Wouldn't that be wonderful?" Her mother
glanced over at Ellie. "You're awfully quiet.
Anything wrong?"

"No . . . I just have some things on my
mind."

"Are you wishing you could live like
Kathy does? If so, I understand. Who
wouldn't want to live like that?"

"No, Mom," Ellie said quietly. "I wouldn't
trade places with Kathy for anything in the
world."

Ten

"Come look at all the presents we got!"
Ellie buried her face in her pillow.
"Geez, Marcy, what time is it anyway?"

"Six-thirty. Time to get up. It's Christmas."

Ellie smelled the aromas of coffee brewing and orange-raisin muffins baking. "Is Mom up?"

"Everybody's up 'cept you." Marcy tugged on Ellie's hand.

"I'm coming," Ellie mumbled sleepily.

By the time she got downstairs, her mother was sitting on the couch, sipping coffee. Marcy was eagerly pawing through the pile of gifts—a far larger pile than Ellie had expected. "Are all these for us?" Ellie asked her mother.

"There are some perks when you work in a department store," her mother said with a laugh. "One is a twenty percent discount."

"Thanks, Mom," Ellie said, realizing that the pile of gifts meant sacrifice, not surplus.

"I know this past year's been rough on you girls, but I love you both and I only want the best for you." She squeezed Ellie's hand.

"This big one's for me!" Marcy said. She pulled out a large box from where Ellie had stashed it behind the tree. "It says it's from Santa." Marcy giggled. "I'm too old for Santa."

"You sure about that?" Ellie asked. "He'd be insulted if he knew you felt that way about him, you know."

Marcy ripped off the paper and squealed. "It's my Barbie apartment! Look! Just what I wanted." She looked at her mother. "Thanks, Mom!"

"It's not from me," their mother said, looking surprised.

"Don't look at me," Ellie said when Marcy turned her way.

"But who . . . ?" Marcy paused. "Oh, who cares? I love it. It's just what I wanted."

Eventually Ellie opened her clock radio, which she'd carefully wrapped and labeled TO ELLIE FROM SANTA. Much later, after all the gifts had been opened and Marcy was playing happily in the living room, Ellie and her mother nibbled on warm muffins at the kitchen table. "That's a nice radio you bought for yourself," Ellie's mother said. "But it isn't the one you told me you were getting. There's no CD player in it."

Ellie shrugged. "I decided I didn't need a CD player. A radio is just fine."

"You bought that toy for Marcy, didn't you?"

"She really wanted it."

"You really wanted that CD clock radio."

Ellie shrugged. "Not as much as I thought I did."

Her mother cupped her hand over Ellie's. "It was kind of you, Ellie. And it makes me proud of you. You're turning into such a fine young woman."

Ellie felt a deep pleasure at her mother'
words. "It's nice to have a family, Mom
Even half of one."

"I love you, Ellie. You and Marcy mea
the world to me. I don't know if your fathe
will ever be a part of your lives again. I hop
he will. He's missing so much by stayin,
away."

Ellie couldn't answer around the lump i
her throat. She took a big swig of milk t
keep from bawling.

Night had come before Ellie made it ove
to Kathy's. She found Kathy sitting on th
dock, looking across the dark water. On th
far side of the lake, houses were ablaze wit
lights, and the faint sounds of Christmas mu
sic drifted on the cool night air. A lamp, se
cured to a post on the dock, cast a pool o
soft yellow light downward, illuminating th
wooden boards. "Hi," Ellie said, sitting be
side Kathy. "I brought some Christma
presents for you and Chris. They're from m
and Marcy." She slid the paper bag she'
been carrying closer to Kathy.

"That's nice of you," Kathy said, fingerin
the bag. "Did you have a good Christmas?

"Yeah, we did. Better than I ever expected. How about you?"

"The Davidsons gave me tons of stuff. And Chris, too. He fell asleep before he even finished opening his gifts."

Ellie smiled, imagining the little boy nodding off over his piles of presents. She reached into the bag. "This is for Chris from Marcy. It's a sock doll that she made herself."

"I'll let him open it tomorrow."

"And I bought him this Nerf soccer ball. I figure he can't do too much damage with it." Ellie reached down into the bag. "And these are for you."

Kathy unwrapped the smaller box first and found a pair of soccer-ball earrings. "Cute," she said.

"Marcy's idea to match up the soccer balls!"

The next box held a beautiful book, its cover decorated with angels. The pages were blank, except for the first one, on which Ellie had written, *The Thoughts and Feelings of Kathy Tolena. Given to her by Ellie Matthias, Christmas Day.* "I thought you might like to keep a journal," she said. "It's supposed to

help you feel better to write down your feelings."

"It's beautiful. Thank you." Kathy
smoothed her palm over the surface of the
book. "I have plenty to write about." She
reached into the pocket of her oversized
sweater and pulled out a small box. "I've
been carrying it around all day. It's for you."

Ellie opened it and discovered a delicate
gold chain on which hung a heart-shaped
locket and a tiny key. "Oh, my gosh! It's so
pretty. Thank you, Kathy."

"I put a picture of Chris inside the locket,"
Kathy said. "And the key is to remind you
not to give your heart away to any guy who
doesn't deserve it."

"Not to worry. It won't happen." Ellie fas-
tened the chain around her neck, took a deep
breath, and asked, "What did you give the
Davidsons?"

"I signed the papers. They're Chris's mom
and dad now."

Tears instantly filled Ellie's eyes. "Are you
sure?"

"I have to do what's best for Chris. I have
to get out of his life while there's still time for
him to forget me. I know it's the right thing

to do for him." Kathy's voice shook. "I made another decision, too. I'm not going back to school in January."

"Oh, Kathy, no—"

"The Davidsons have already tried to talk me into staying, but this is what I want to do. I've outgrown high school anyway."

Ellie understood perfectly. Because of what she'd been through, Kathy was old beyond her years.

"What about your diploma?"

"I can take exams, and if I pass the tests I'll get the diploma anyway. It's done all the time."

"But June's only six months away." Ellie didn't want Kathy to leave.

"I have to get out of here, Ellie. If Pam's really going to be Chris's mother, then I can't be hanging around, now can I?" Kathy took a shuddering breath. "I'm going to Kuwait and stay with my parents . . . just for a while. Until I figure out what to do with the rest of my life."

"You're Chris's mother. How can you give him up?"

"Because I love him. Because he deserves more than I can give him."

"But—"

"I've made up my mind. Please don't make it any harder by trying to talk me out of it."

"Chris won't know you—"

"Pam says she'll tell him he's adopted. She says that if he ever asks—*when* he asks—she'll tell him all about me and show him pictures of the two of us. She'll tell him how much I loved him and how I took care of him when he was only a baby. And I've written a long letter for Pam to show him when he asks why I gave him away. I've read about adopted kids who worry about that. I want him to know I love him, but that I couldn't keep him. I don't ever want him to hate me."

"Well, you tell him to contact me and I'll tell him the truth, too," Ellie announced, fighting back tears.

"Thanks. Maybe I will."

"Wh-When are you leaving?"

"In a couple of days. I need to make a quick, clean break."

"W-Will you write me?"

"I will. You're a good friend, Ellie."

The tears in Ellie's eyes made the lights across the lake blur. She looked up. The stars looked like glittering seeds spread across a black field, sown by God the way a child scatters jacks. "I'll always keep your secret. I promise by the light of the stars."

"Thank you for that."

Ellie said, "You'll be with Chris again, Kathy. No matter how far away you go, no matter who raises him . . you'll find each other again one day. Just like the light from those stars finds its way down to us."

Together, their shoulders touching, she and Kathy sat on the end of the dock, gazing up at the starry, starry night.

Epilogue

The stars have been shining above us forever: the North Star, which guided sailors on their tall ships; the star of wonder, which led wise men across a desert toward a newborn child. The stars peek and gleam at us through the majestic night sky.

They lead.

They guide.

They unite strangers, loved ones, the lost, the lonely, the hopeful.

They hear wishes, too.

Select your own star. There's a wishing star for everyone. Take time this very night to look up with an open heart and make your own wish, dream your own dream.

Just repeat these words:

> *Star light, star bright,*
> *First star I see tonight,*
> *I wish I may, I wish I might*
> *Have the wish I wish tonight.*

For wishes and dreams can come true. We all—strangers, loved ones, the lost, the lonely, the hopeful—can be one family, on one planet, in one galaxy, in one universe. We belong to one another. And to the stars.

LURLENE McDANIEL began writing inspirational novels about teenagers facing life-altering situations when her son was diagnosed with juvenile diabetes. "I saw first-hand how chronic illness affects every aspect of a person's life," she has said. "I want kids to know that while people don't get to choose what life gives to them, they do get to choose how to respond."

Lurlene McDaniel's novels are hard-hitting and realistic, but also leave readers with inspiration and hope. Her books have received acclaim from readers, teachers, parents, and reviewers. Her recent novels *Angels Watching Over Me*, and its companion *Lifted Up by Angels*, as well as *Don't Die, My Love* and *I'll Be Seeing You*, have all been national bestsellers. *Six Months to Live* was included in a literary time capsule at the Library of Congress in Washington, D.C.

Lurlene McDaniel's other popular Bantam novels include *Till Death Do Us Part; For Better, for Worse, Forever; Too Young to Die; Goodbye Doesn't Mean Forever; Somewhere Between Life and Death; Time to Let Go; Now I Lay Me Down to Sleep; When Happily Ever After Ends; Baby Alicia Is Dying;* and the One Last Wish novels: *A Time to Die; Mourning Song; Mother, Help Me Live; Someone Dies, Someone Lives; Sixteen and Dying; Let Him Live; The Legacy: Making Wishes Come True; Please Don't Die; She Died Too Young; All the Days of Her Life;* and *A Season for Goodbye.*

Lurlene McDaniel lives in Chattanooga, Tennessee.